Sword of Light

The Four Keys, Volume 1

J.C. Lucas

Published by J.C. Lucas, 2020.

Cover Art by Maria Spada

Dedication
For my Mom, Grandmother, and Meme. Thank you for help-
ing me to realize my dreams, to indulge me in my passions,
and for always having faith in me

Chapter One

At sixteen, I didn't expect to have to deal with another death in the family. Even in my wildest dreams, I never imagined I would be sitting in a social worker's office, waiting to be taken to a new home. Yet here I was, a week after my nan died, with no family, no close friends, and no idea what my future holds.

Fiddling with the strap on my bag, I looked around the mundane office wondering where the social worker had gone off to this time.

Anne had swooped in the same day that the ambulance took Nan to the hospital. She had picked me up from school and rushed me to Nan's side, just as she took her final breath. I held onto her cold hand for hours, numbness taking over before Anne finally pried me away.

She pulled me from the hospital room, murmuring nonsensical words to me, but I hadn't paid any attention. I stared back at Nan as we walked away, my heart a heavy lump in my chest, my eyes burning from the tears that I had shed.

It was at that moment, as Anne shuffled me away from the woman who had raised me, that I noticed soft lights swirling around her body, faster and faster through the air until they disappeared. At the moment, I had chalked it up to distress, exhaustion, and maybe the headache that had been pounding behind my eyes. But as I sat here now, thinking back on that day, I was sure that I hadn't imagined them.

Anne strolled around the corner, a tall man following behind her. He wore a suit and tie and carried a fancy briefcase. His stature next to Anne's shorter one made her appear as if she were only four feet tall.

The guy, who looked a little like the used car salesman who always ran cheesy ads on TV, raised his eyebrows as he looked me over before dismissing me to once again chat with her.

I really didn't care who he was, but his response irritated me for reasons I didn't understand. Fear about what would happen rippled through my body. Would the slimy-looking man take me somewhere I didn't want to go? My breath came quicker as anxiety began to set in. It seemed to happen a lot lately. It made me lightheaded, my chest tight, and caused me to feel as if I were spiraling out of control.

Gritting my teeth, I resolved to be tough and tamped down the cold feeling, putting it away in its own little box. I would get through whatever was next by myself. I didn't need anyone.

Chapter Two

Curling up in the backseat as close to the car door as possible, I couldn't help but stare at Anne as she talked to herself. She kept looking over at her purse, giggling and shaking her head. *She's so weird....* A few days ago, I decided that she must have a screw loose or some kind of chemical imbalance.

Her laughter made my ears burn now, and rage festered inside me. How could she be happy when my world had been torn apart? She could at least try to act like she cared that Nan died. Why couldn't she put herself in my place and see how horrible it felt for me to leave my home? Here I was, going to live with someone I had never met before, and she was laughing! I couldn't believe how insensitive she was.

Narrowing my eyes, I stared daggers at the back of her head.

The rain picked up as we sped down the highway to Junction, and outside the window, tall trees obscured everything else. They were so different from the trees back home. Not at all like the red cedar or spindly pecan trees that dotted the landscape in North Texas. These trees soared high into the sky, growing so thick together that it was impossible to see through them. Huge oaks and towering pines grew together in masses. What would it be like to climb to the top of one and sit so high above the rest of the world? I imagined myself up there, screaming my anger at the world. It might at least make me feel better for a little while.

"Andie, are you doing okay back there?"

I glanced at Anne and caught her looking at me in the rearview mirror with wide green eyes. Remaining silent, I gave her a blank stare as she looked back at me, her eyes scanning mine in the mirror. I was furious that she even dared to talk to me. She should be used to this by now. Not once had I responded to her since she picked me up, and I wasn't about to this time. Who did she think she was? She didn't care, not for one minute.

Huffing, I turned away from her to gaze out the rain-streaked window again. She probably thought I was a brat. And honestly? I didn't care.

Anne turned the car onto a dirt road lined with more trees, and we bumped down the rock drive. At the end, tucked away with tall trees appeared a small white house. Flowers of every color decorated the landscape, brightening the dreary day. As the car pulled up in front of the house, there were no other homes visible from where I sat. The surrounding woods encased the home, and trees were all I could see for miles.

This place was so different than what I was used to. Nan's house had been in a suburb, with cookie-cutter homes. Each one had been the same, side-by-side with no yard to speak of. I was never fond of the proximity between them and rarely opened the curtains in my bedroom for fear that the next-door neighbor might look in. I wouldn't have to worry about any neighbors here, that was for sure.

"Andie, I know you don't want to be here, but Celeste was your Nan's friend and she agreed to take you in. This place will grow on you, I promise. There's so much waiting for you here."

Again, she peered at me in the rearview mirror, and I shrugged, looking away from her while she lumbered out of the car. She was short and broad but carried herself as if she were a six-foot-tall duchess. Her long brown ponytail swayed in time with her hips.

I sat in the backseat with my arms crossed, watching her before looking over what was to be my new home.

The screen door at the top of the porch opened and an older woman wearing a long blue skirt and a flowing white shirt stepped outside. Her gray hair was long and braided, her face remarkably unlined for someone her age. *Must be good genes,* I thought, curious about the lady I would live with. She glanced at me, smirking as if she was aware of some inside joke that I wasn't privy to.

Walking over to Anne, she wrapped her in a hug.

I wonder how they knew each other. The familiarity between the two made it seem as if they were friends. They spoke for a moment before the woman patted Anne on the shoulder and headed over to the car. Opening the back door, she leaned down to look at me with eyes that were a bright sapphire blue and seemed to see into my very soul.

"Hi, Andie. It's so good to finally meet you. I'm Celeste. Won't you come inside so we can visit for a bit and get better acquainted? I've been awaiting your arrival all day."

She smiled warmly and seemed genuinely happy that I was there. It seemed strange that someone would willingly open their home to a sixteen-year-old teenager who they'd never met before. For all she knew, I could be a serial killer or a thief who would rob her blind.

She reached inside the car, her face relaxed and her eyes sparkling. I did not doubt that Anne had told her all about my crummy attitude, so it surprised me that she seemed so accepting. Glancing down at her hand, I hesitantly grasped it with my own. Warmth raced up my arm, and a tingling peacefulness took over, easing the tension in my body. Baffled by it, I pondered where it came from.

I unfolded myself from the backseat, stepping out of the car. Anne already had my bags in both hands and my backpack slung over her broad shoulders as she shuffled to the steps.

Celeste continued to hold my hand as she led us up to the porch, the strange warmth racing from her hand to mine. I was floating in the cozy feeling as we walked up, and I felt too tired to question it.

Looking around the porch, I spotted a sign by the door that stated, "Haven." Those words hit me hard in the gut, tugging at emotions I had kept bottled up for the last few days. Heck, the last week since Nan passed. She had always been my *Haven*. My safe place, the one I always thought would be there for me. Losing Nan was the hardest thing I had ever been through in my life.

I never wanted to feel like that again.

I couldn't remember either of my parents. Mom died when I was two, and my father disappeared soon after. No one knew what had become of him. Not a single letter was sent. Not a payment made on any of his credit cards. Everyone just assumed he was dead.

Nan had been the one constant in my life, and like any teenager, I had taken for granted she would be around forever. My chest ached and tears pooled in my eyes, so fresh was the pain from her loss. I turned my head away from Anne and Celeste to hide my despair. I couldn't bear for anyone to witness my pain.

As if sensing what I tried to hide, Celeste squeezed my hand a few times before gently letting it go to usher us into the living room. It was bright, with a ton of plants scattered around. The greenery gave the room a clean and peaceful vibe. A sofa sat in the middle of the room, looking worn but comfortable with blankets draped over the back, and knickknacks littered various side tables. What caught my eye, though, was a bookcase covering an entire wall, floor-to-ceiling, with every shelf full of books.

Celeste and Anne talked, but their voices became only background noise as I wandered over to the gorgeous bookcase, running my fingers over the spines of classics and old books I had never seen before. It was amazing! My love of books and my despair at having to leave all my favorites behind was completely and utterly washed away by seeing this wonderful display.

Nan always said I had an old soul. She indulged my love of books and would take me on a weekly trip to the local bookstore to let me pick out one book each time. I was always cautious, taking my time to make sure the book I picked out was one I would read and enjoy multiple times. It had to fuel my imagination and draw me in so much that I got lost in the story, imagining I was part of the adventure. For the most part, every book I got did just that. I'm sure some people would say I'm a nerd, but I wouldn't care. A lot of the time, I found that reading books was better than being around most people.

Looking at all the different titles, I noted which books I wanted to read while I was here. The books were a bright spot in this situation. But Celeste and Anne didn't need to know that. I hoped if I were enough of a brat, they'd return me to my old home, as silly as that hope might be.

Scowling, I turned around and plopped down in the most unladylike manner possible, causing Celeste to raise her eyebrows. She studied me but surprisingly made no mention of my rudeness.

Walking over, she and Anne sat down, both watching me, perhaps waiting for an outburst. I rolled my eyes, staring at the books in front of me. I would not give them the satisfaction.

Celeste cleared her throat, breaking the silence. "Becca—well, your nan, was an extraordinary friend. We met when we were young girls. You remind me so much of her. It's uncanny! Even though I hadn't seen her in years, we wrote to each other as much as possible. So many of her letters were about you and how much joy you brought her. One day, I'll let you read them if you like. You were her entire world. I understand that you're having a tough time, but I hope you'll let me help you get through this."

My stomach clenched as I pushed down the feelings her kind words evoked in me. My emotions were all over the board, and I didn't want to be that weepy girl everyone pitied.

Toying with the fringe from the blanket hanging over the back of the couch, I tried my hardest to act indifferent. I didn't want Celeste to know I was hanging on to her every word.

The women shared a knowing look and rose to walk together toward the front door. They murmured to each other for a while, but no matter how hard I strained, I couldn't make out what they were saying. Anne turned back, talking to herself again, and looked around the room.

What was she up to now?

Spying a book lying on an end table, she exclaimed, "AHH, there you are! Don't be stealing my thunder again!"

She gave the book a crazy evil eye, and I tried to figure out what the heck she was going on about. Gazing back at me, she smiled, wiggled her eyebrows, then snorted before turning away to walk outside with Celeste, leaving me bewildered.

Staring at the book, I tried to make sense of what I had witnessed. The book was thick and covered in brown leather, the title not visible as the backside of the book was face up. Looked like a normal book to me, albeit an old one.

Shaking my head, I stood up from the couch, stretching my arms above my head to relieve the tension in my shoulders. A strange noise came from the next room, and I lowered my arms to listen.

What was that?

The sound drifted through the air again, and I realized it was someone whistling. Curious, I followed the sound into a sunroom filled with different plants and flowers. Some were regular houseplants, and others were tropical. The sweetness of jasmine permeated the room, tickling my nose. The whistling grew much louder as I walked around a pair of tall bamboo plants.

And there it was. A birdcage with a beautiful blue parrot swinging on a perch, whistling its heart out. The parrot's eyes were closed as it whistled, while it swung back and forth on the little wooden swing. It seemed content, and happiness rippled off its feathers. A giggle rose in my throat before bubbling out at the funny picture the bird made. I slapped my hand over my mouth to muffle the sound.

I shouldn't be happy—definitely not giggling! I frowned at the parrot for making me laugh, as if it had done it on purpose. Opening its eyes, the bird cocked its head and squawked at me.

"Hello!"

Its eyes were wide and staring at me as if it were waiting for me to say something back. Staying silent, I watched it tilt its little head side to side and step from foot to foot.

"Hellooo!"

The volume of the screech startled me, and I jumped high in the air, putting a hand to my chest as my heart beat erratically. Jeez! This bird has some lungs!

"I see you've met Charlie." Celeste glided into the room, smiling fondly at the parrot. "He found his way here with a hurt wing, and I did my best to heal him. We've been friends ever since, and let me tell you, he keeps me on my toes. Charlie is quite the chatterbox, and it's always a mystery what he will say next." Walking over to the cage, she leaned in as Charlie leaned forward, and she kissed the tip of his beak.

"Love you, love you!" The bird sang to her, preening from side to side. He turned his head to look at me as if expecting me to kiss him too. *Nope. Not going to happen.* His skills were impressive and all, but kissing a bird is not my thing. Shaking my head, I gave him a disgusted look before walking over to the large windows to gaze at the surrounding woods. Chatty Charlie prattled on in the background as I looked out.

I had never seen so many tall trees in one place. The woods were thick, and the darkness called out to me, promising solitude and an escape from reality. I couldn't wait to explore. It was strange, but there seemed to be a pull on my soul to go there now.

Celeste called to me and I shook the strange feeling off. She must have said my name a few times, trying to get my attention.

"Dear, are you all right? You were lost in your thoughts. Why don't we go upstairs, and I'll show you your room? Then we can have some tea and chat awhile. Or if you prefer, you can rest a bit. Whatever you'd like." She gestured to me, and I quietly followed her through the house to the stairs.

Halfway up, art hanging along the wall caught my eyes, and I stopped to study one of the paintings. It was a picture of the night sky filled with stars painted so beautifully that it was as if they really twinkled. Underneath the diamond-laden sky lay a green forest with small golden lights sprinkled throughout the trees. Fairies peeked out between leaves, as others danced around a circle of stones on the ground below. Each one wore delicate dresses made of flowers, and tiny slippers made of leaves. Inside the circle of stones sat a book with a glowing symbol gracing the cover. The ethereal quality of the painting was stunning. Whoever had painted it was exceptionally talented.

We continued up the stairs. The bedroom Celeste brought me to was gorgeous, and I mumbled as much as I walked around. A small white desk sat under a large picture window, with writing instruments and paper laid out. I imagined myself sitting there on a beautiful day, writing, doing homework, and looking out the window. At night, I would watch the moon shine down on the top of the great oaks. A full-size wrought iron bed rested against the wall, the coverlet, white with tiny blackbirds, and pillows were piled high. I longed to jump on the softness of them and wallow around.

Celeste also showed me the adjoining bathroom, which was small, but a good size for me. Toiletries, makeup, and a new toothbrush sat by the sink. She had thought of everything I might need. Even though I wanted to go home, this place didn't seem too bad.

"I'll leave you here to unpack your things and get comfortable with your new room. If there's anything you think of that you need, please tell me. We can run to town anytime you like, and tomorrow we head that way to get you enrolled in school. Come on down when you're ready, and I'll fix us a nice cup of hot tea." Celeste smiled before shutting the door behind her.

Ugh, school.

I didn't even want to think about going to a new school. It gave me anxiety, worrying about how everyone would treat me, the new girl. I had friends back at Central High, but no one I had been really close to. So many of the kids at my old school were entitled brats. Their parents bought them anything they could ever want, not what they needed. They were only friends with other kids just like them, who were obsessed with themselves and changed friends on a whim. I had always tried to steer clear of them. Who wanted friends like that?

Definitely not me.

After putting my meager belongings away, the closet still looked empty. My wardrobe only comprised of jeans, old T-shirts, cardigans, and my favorite Converse tennis shoes. I didn't care about clothes and what was "in style." I liked being comfortable and having my own look; Nan had always encouraged me to be myself. So that's what I did. She used to tell me how "cute" I looked in my beanie and glasses. I had yet to find any reason to try contacts. The thought of sticking something in my eyes grossed me out, and I wasn't ready to submit myself to that torture.

My beanie was the one thing I would never give up. It was a tried-and-true staple of my wardrobe, no matter what the weather was, and no matter what I was wearing. I found it in Nan's hope chest when I was nine. When she told me it had been my mom's, my nine-year-old self had clung to that beanie and wore it every day. It was my security blanket from that moment on. It's silly, but somehow, I felt by wearing it, it somehow made me closer to the woman I had never known.

Making my way downstairs, I followed the smell of cookies until I found myself in the kitchen. Celeste sat at a table, sipping a mug of tea and reading the same book that crazy Anne had been talking to. I eyed it warily, half-expecting some monster or genie to jump out. When she heard me enter, Celeste closed the book and set it aside, face down.

"Would you like some green tea, Andie? I've got some in the teapot."

Nodding, I sat down on a barstool by the kitchen island, swinging my feet as I looked around the room. It was clean and comfortable, with herbs lined up in pots on a shelf, and cookies cooling on a rack, their aroma floating through the air. Taking a deep breath, I savored it. That delicious aroma was familiar, and memories of making the cookies with Nan made my heart twinge.

"Here's your tea. I made snickerdoodles. I think I remember your Nan telling me she always made them for you. I hope they're as good as hers."

No one baked snickerdoodles as good as Nan.

A lump of sorrow welled up in my throat, and I swallowed hard to force it down. It didn't work very well, so I sipped the hot tea and stuffed a cookie in my mouth. Hopefully, she didn't notice the emotion on my face; Nan also said I would never make a good poker player.

I chewed the cookie, marveling at how they tasted so much like the ones I grew up eating. I wondered if Nan had shared her recipe with Celeste. Swiveling my chair around to face her as she took a seat at the table, she was studying me, not critically, but with patience and understanding. She was waiting for me to speak up; I could tell from the look in her eyes. So I did.

"Celeste, how did you and Nan meet? I don't remember her ever talking about you, which seems kinda strange if you were such good friends. Maybe I wasn't paying attention, but since I'm supposed to live here with you, I think it's fair to ask."

She smiled and began her story.

"Your nan and I met when we were both around your age. She had a vibrant soul, full of energy and curiosity. Somehow, she got lost in these very woods one evening. I was out there too and came upon her as she was trying to find her way home. Oh, she looked a right mess with grass in her brown hair, her knees dirty from stumbling a time or two. She was so grateful, and she held onto me the entire time I was leading her home. From that moment on, we were fast friends. We fought a lot of life's battles together in our younger years, and we were inseparable until she met your grandfather. That's when we drifted apart. We wrote to each other for years, sharing heartaches and happiness. I also visited her once when your grandfather passed away. It was a nice visit, but she was distraught and had a lot going on so I didn't stay long. There were a lot of important things she had to take care of, and I understood..." Celeste drifted off, a faraway look in her eyes as if lost in thoughts of the past.

She had a way of making things sound so mysterious, which only made me want to press for more information. I wanted to know more about Nan and her life that I was never privy to before, but Celeste had closed the conversation. I would just have to wait.

We discussed the school I would be going to, and Celeste went on and on about it. She thought it was a great school. Time would tell. We were going there tomorrow and she would sign me up to be a student. My stomach clenched at the thought. She also mentioned we would stop at the store to pick up whatever supplies I might need, and she wanted to take me to lunch at a café one of her friends owned. She raved about the food and how much she thought I would enjoy it.

With all the talk about what we would do, I warmed a little to the idea and looked forward to a normal day. Once the sun set, we had a small dinner consisting of salad and warm bread. It was simple but good, and I relaxed more than I had in a while, enjoying her quiet companionship. I was grateful she didn't push me into talking about how I was coping with everything. Right now, I just couldn't talk about it without getting emotional, or angry.

Not long after, I headed up to bed, hoping to sleep without the regular nightmares appearing. As I lay down on the pillowy softness of my new bed, sleep dragged me under.

Running through the dark woods, fear overtook me. Heavy footfalls caught up and had my stomach clenching in horror. I pushed my legs to go faster, and my breath crystallized in the air as I panted from exertion. Frantic, I couldn't stop. I knew it would kill me. I dodged through trees that displayed four-point stars with twisted knots inside of them glowing on their rough bark. The sight of those stars burned into my brain, and somehow, I knew they were important.

Moist breath whispered over the back of my neck, reminding me I didn't have time to worry about the symbols. Whatever was chasing me had caught up, and the terror I felt was overwhelming. Tumbling, I fell to my knees, rolling over to jump up to face my pursuer. My eyes widened, and my mouth fell open in horror as I stared at a giant man standing menacingly in front of me.

Pale white skin stood stark in contrast to the midnight black of his armor. He sneered down at me, and jagged teeth filled his mouth as saliva dripped from the corners. Lifting a razor-sharp spear high in the air, a hideous noise sounded low in his throat, and soulless black eyes pierced me. My body moved as if it already knew what to do. Like a puppet on a string, I jumped with feet raised, kicking my legs hard into his chest. The hit catapulted him through the dark woods, his body disappearing into the forest while all the glowing symbols on the trees dimmed and faded.

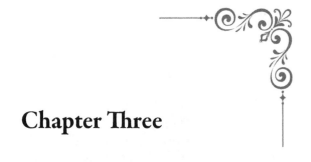

Chapter Three

Rolling over onto my side and stretching, I opened my eyes to see the sunlight filtering in through the curtains while the remains of the dream left me feeling confused. The great oaks swayed in the breeze while Pachelbel's Canon played through the earbuds that lay on the bed beside me. *Ugh.* I had pulled them out during the night. No wonder I had that horrible dream. I always went to sleep with my earbuds in and classical music playing. It was the only way I could go to sleep and stay asleep. That is, if they *stayed* in my ears.

Nan had suggested music long ago when my nightmares began. She had known it would keep the dreams at bay. There had been plenty of nights she would have to wake me up because my night terrors were so bad. Many times, after she woke me, she would rock me in her arms with soothing words spilling from her mouth. Her eyes were always troubled, and I wasn't sure if she tried to soothe me or herself.

Glancing one more time out the window, I tossed the earbuds on the nightstand before making myself roll out of bed to prepare for the day. It was seven in the morning, and while we didn't have a set time to be at the school, I wanted to get our visit to town done as early as possible. While putting my shoes on, Celeste called my name from the bottom of the stairs, asking if I was ready to go.

"I'll be down in a minute," I grumbled and headed down to meet her.

The drive to town took fifteen minutes. I hadn't realized how far out in the country the house was. The winding roads had trees bowing over them, making it feel as though we drove through a tunnel of nature, and everywhere I looked, the landscape was green with wildflowers scattered across the ground.

We arrived in town, and it was *small*. There was one main street going through town, with shops and restaurants lined up and down. The school loomed at the end of the road, with only three different old gray buildings. Elementary, middle, and high school shared the same campus. And let me tell you, they didn't seem like the warmest or most welcoming looking buildings either.

"Here we are, Andie. Let's get you signed up!" Celeste seemed cheery as she parked the car, and we got out.

Me? Not so much.

Heading to the front door, we walked inside just as the bell rang. Doors in the hallway were flung open with a flood of teenagers barreling out and heading in every direction. Grabbing my hand, she led me to the office, where bulletins were posted on the window for different events. One caught my eye. "Moonlight and Magic." The flyer stated the school would hold the event on April 25th. There were dragons, dwarves, castles, and unicorns gracing the flyer. Was it a dance, or a carnival? I knew I'd have to find out more. Anything involving mythical creatures was right up my alley.

I didn't have much time to think about it before Celeste introduced me to the secretary, Mrs. Simpson. We chatted for a moment and then signed all the papers. I held a class list and a supply list gathered to my chest before I even realized it. Celeste talked for a while with Mrs. Simpson, and growing bored, I leaned my head back against the wall, stared at the floor, and wished they would hurry.

As I concentrated on a piece of dirt on the linoleum floor, something scurried fast as lightning under the office door. Right after, the door crashed open, bouncing off the wall with a loud bang, and a tall boy lunged inside, panting as his head moved in every direction. He smoothed back the caramel-colored hair that had fallen into his eyes, looking at the three of us with a flash of embarrassment in his eyes.

"I'm so sorry, Mrs. Simpson. Harvey escaped his cage again, and I was trying to catch him for Mr. Timmons." He looked at me with curiosity.

Mrs. Simpson nodded and smirked like this happened every day. She wasn't surprised at all. "Teagan, you scared the daylights out of our visitors here. Ladies, this is Teagan King. He's a junior here at Junction and is the only one who can ever catch Harvey when he gets out. Which happens daily." She laughed and waved at Teagan to go get Harvey, a tiny white mouse huddled up against a bookbag in the room's corner.

Poor thing. I would want to escape too if I were locked up all the time too. I studied Teagan as he moved toward Harvey with slow, steady steps. Kneeling, he scooped up the little mouse in both of his palms, bringing them cupped to his chest as he cradled the tiny creature. The mouse wasn't scared of Teagan and didn't try to run away.

Amazing!

As he looked up from his hands, I saw that his eyes were dark gray, with thick black eyelashes any girl would die for. The depth I saw in them as they pierced into my own mesmerized me. Shaking myself, I broke the stare, embarrassed.

"That's awesome how he let you pick him up like that." I pushed my glasses further up my nose in a nervous habit while he grinned back at me, his eyes crinkling at the corners. I thought he had a nice smile and seemed friendly.

Clearing her throat, Mrs. Simpson smiled and introduced us. "Teagan, this is Andie and Celeste. Andie will start school here tomorrow. She's a junior too. I hope you'll help make her feel at home."

"Nice to meet you both! Andie, if you want to, you can meet me here by the office tomorrow morning. I can show you where your classes are."

His kindness surprised me, and I stammered.

"Uh... um, yeah, sounds like a plan. Thank you."

Ugh, that sounded so stupid. I wanted to slap myself for sounding like such a loser. My cheeks heated, and I could feel them turn bright red.

He only gave a lopsided grin as he waved to us before turning to exit the office. "See ya tomorrow, Andie!" he called over his shoulder.

After leaving the school, we stopped at multiple stores, buying all the supplies I needed and marking them off the list. Then she took me to a small boutique in town and bought me a few new pairs of jeans. I protested at the frou-frou shirts she tried to coax me to try on, making sure she understood I thought my T-shirts were just fine. She shook her head at me, but I caught the smile as she turned away. She reminded me a lot of Nan.

Once done shopping, we stopped at the café for a late lunch, and I met her friend Sari. She was a hardened older lady who didn't fit the typical picture of a small-town café owner. Sari had a purple pixie cut and wore all black leather, and I thought her nose ring was cool. I wondered what I would look like with a little stud in my nose. I couldn't pull it off like she could, though I longed to look a little more badass. But first I guess I would actually have to *be* a badass to pull it off. I was far from that.

Sari was funny, and her sarcastic attitude endeared her to me. She cracked jokes and instantly made me feel at home. She was great, and I already wanted to get to know her better. Maybe after I got my driver's license, I would see if she needed any help at the café. I could use a job to save up money. I couldn't live with Celeste forever.

I studied Sari as she went behind the counter to help some customers while we ate our lunch. Celeste ate a fantastic-looking chicken salad, and I had decided on a juicy burger and fries that made my taste buds tingle. I almost moaned at the first bite, savoring and enjoying the flavors. Once I finished my meal, I sat back, patting my full stomach, satisfied like I couldn't ever remember being. Several other customers were doing the same. Satisfaction radiated from them, and I found it humorous and mind-boggling at the same time. Sari looked at me from over the counter, a glimmer of mischief in her eyes, and she winked before going back into the kitchen.

Interesting.

Excusing myself from the table, I went to find the bathroom at the back of the café. As I reached for the door, a woman with long black hair and dark eyes yanked it open, bumping my shoulder on her way out. I apologized after stepping out of her way and rubbed my shoulder where she had hit it.

Stopping in her tracks, she looked me up and down, her eyes flashing fire. Her perfect features screwed into a frown as she leaned forward, sniffing the air around me. My back stiffened, and the hairs on my neck rose. *What the heck?*

I shifted backwards, trying to distance myself from her as best I could in the small hallway. Never had anyone been rude enough to actually smell me. What she was doing wasn't normal, and it ticked me off. Before I had a chance to say anything to her, she sneered, taking a step back with her hands on her hips. The woman stared into my eyes with clear menace, her perfect eyebrow arched and deep red lips pursed.

"You are weak! I can't imagine what they see in YOU!"

She spat at me as if I were the most disgusting thing she had ever seen, and then murmured strange words under her breath, throwing her hands up in the air between us. I swear her eyes glowed, but it had to have been a trick of the light. My hair ruffled with a slight breeze, but there were no fans inside the diner that could have caused it. Standing there in shock, I tried to figure out what this lunatic was doing.

The woman lowered her arms, her brow sinking as she scowled at me. She looked me up and down one more time before stomping off with her heels clicking on the tile.

My feet were planted to the floor as I looked after her. Something about the way she had acted gave me the chills.

Disturbed by what happened, I shook the ominous feeling off as best I could and walked back to our table, not saying a word to Sari or Celeste about the encounter. They wouldn't believe me anyway and would probably assume I had somehow caused the trouble.

Later, we pulled into the driveway as dusk set atop the trees, casting light beams over the ground and taking my breath away at the beauty. I realized right then that the country was much better than the city, if not just for the views. When the car stopped outside the house, I caught movement out of the corner of my eye. Turning to look out the window, a boy, maybe twelve years old, looked back at me from the edge of the thick forest. He was smiling ear to ear, then bowed at the waist with a sweep of his arm.

I looked back at Celeste, exclaiming as I pointed out the window. "Who is that!?"

Confusion showed in her eyes as she looked where I was pointing. Turning back, I saw that the boy had disappeared. Celeste scanned the area before gazing at me again, shrugging her delicate shoulders.

"He was there! He must have run into the woods."

She looked skeptical and patted my shoulder. Was she patronizing me? That frustrated me to no end.

"Look. I really saw him, I swear!" Throwing the door open, I scrambled out of the car, running over to the edge of the trees where he had been standing.

"Andie, why don't you explore a little? Fresh air might do you some good," Celeste said.

I continued to scan the forest for some sign of the kid. He couldn't have gone too far. Celeste went into the house with our packages, not concerned at all, and I gritted my teeth, struggling to control my temper. I may have been just a teenager, but I wasn't crazy!

As I strolled along the tree line, close to where I had seen the boy, something caught the fading light from the sun, glinting in the grass. Stepping closer, I bent down to look.

A skeleton key! It was small, almost the size of a quarter. Picking up the key, I studied it with wonder. In my palm, it was warm and heavy for its size. Where could it have come from? Was this something the boy had dropped as he ran off? Shoving it into my pocket, I continued to walk around the exterior of the woods.

If the key was his, and he realized he had lost it, I knew he would be back.

Somewhere deep in the trees, an owl hooted, and small animals skittered through leaves and branches. I marveled at the sounds of nature surrounding me as I made my way to the patio.

Wooden Adirondack chairs surrounded a fire pit, perfect for sitting in while reading a book late in the evening. Pulling my legs up as I sat, I hugged my knees to my chest and stared at the clear sky, sighing at the beauty of the stars. Never would I have seen an atmosphere like this in the city with all the bright lights drowning them out. I wondered why Nan moved away from here. With her love of nature, I couldn't imagine how she enjoyed the noise and pollution of the city over the beauty here.

Celeste called to me a while later, announcing dinner, and I stood up from the chair, taking one last look at the dark woods before heading inside. I would love nothing more than to sit out here all night long.

Ambling into the kitchen, I could hear Charlie in the other room. Celeste hadn't been kidding when she said he was a chatterbox. He went on and on as if he was having a full-blown conversation with someone. With the door to the sunroom closed, I couldn't make out what he was tittering about other than hearing him say, "No, not that."

Such a strange bird.

Our meal was a quiet one, and I was lost in thought about school tomorrow. I just wanted to get the first day over with, so I knew what to expect going forward.

After eating, I helped Celeste with the dishes and then wandered off to pick out a book from her library. I thought reading would help me relax enough to go to sleep tonight. I chose one of my favorites, *Gone with the Wind*, and went up to bed.

The air was thick, and an eggy smell permeated the air as I walked through the crumbling hallway of an old house, frantically pushing cobwebs off as they clung to my face. As I reached the end of the hall, the air turned freezing cold, and the room in front of me was splashed with blood and gore. My stomach turned at the sight, and I opened my mouth to scream. No sound came out. It was as if something were squeezing my vocal cords tight. A creature huddled in the corner, ready to spring at me and mix my blood with the others whose body parts lay strewn all over. I choked on the fetid air, and my feet wouldn't move as the creature shuffled closer. It was shorter than me, with gray-scaled skin and horns that stuck out from a misshapen head. Drool dripped from its foul mouth as razor-sharp teeth snapped when it got within a foot of me, a machete-like knife held in its long-fingered grasp. Terror like I had never felt before engulfed me, and then the creature lunged for me.

I can't breathe—I can't breathe!

I was frantic, trying to tear away from the creature, clawing as it wrapped around me, and my eyes snapped open in horror. My hand hit something hard, and I winced at the pain. It took me a minute to realize I had fallen out of the bed and my sheets were tangled all around me. Wrestling them off, I tried to slow my panicked breathing. I pressed my cheek to the cold wood floor, chanting over and over to myself that it was just a nightmare. My heart rate finally returned to normal, and I could think straight again, but I felt terror just the same.

The clock on the nightstand showed it was six in the morning. I hadn't planned on waking up so early for school, but there was no way

I could go back to sleep now. My earbuds were still in, but silent. I grabbed my iPod off the nightstand only to see that the battery was dead. Strange. I had just charged it yesterday. Sighing, I slammed it back down, frustrated. The best way I could rid myself of the lingering fright from the nightmare was to charge ahead and get on with my day.

After showering and getting ready for school, I packed my backpack with all I thought I would need. Braiding my hair and putting my beanie on, I went downstairs to make an English muffin for breakfast. As I descended the stairs, I could hear Charlie. This morning, he was singing in his cheerful bird voice as if only to me, knowing I needed something to lift my crummy mood.

"Good morning to you! Good morning to you!"

It was incredible that every time he spoke, it was always something different. I wondered if Celeste taught him a new phrase to say each day. Now that would be talent for a bird to pick up something so fast. I added teaching him something funny to my to-do list. I thought it would be hilarious and would catch Celeste off guard.

Speaking of Celeste, she was sitting at the table when I walked into the kitchen and reading that same book again. Every time I walked in to find her reading it, she would place it face down, like she was hiding something. Almost as if she didn't want me to see the cover.

Still feeling the aftereffects of the dream, I knew I'd follow the same pattern as I always did. I would be snarky, maybe a little mean. I couldn't help it because the dream last night had really gotten to me. My ugly side comes out when I try desperately to hide how shaken I am. I don't want anyone to know about the nightmares. Like a defense mechanism, it automatically kicked in. What if they told me I needed to see a therapist, or if they thought something was wrong with me? That would be the icing on the cake.

"What's up with the book, Celeste? Is it some trashy old romance you don't want me to know you're reading? You always turn it over when I come in."

I knew how rude it sounded, and a little part of me felt terrible as I got the English muffin and toasted it. Looking over at me, she wasn't fazed at all by my attitude, although she looked amused. Her reaction only fueled my combative attitude. I didn't want her to be amused; I wanted her to get mad. Not because I really *wanted* her to be mad, but because I didn't want her to be kind to me and cause the walls I had built to crumble. I needed all the resolve I could to get through this day.

I huffed as I poured a glass of orange juice.

"No, Andie. It's not some steamy romance I don't want you to know I'm reading. If I were reading one of those, I wouldn't care who knew. No... This book is ancient, full of tales so wild you wouldn't believe it. Stories of magical creatures and different worlds. Full of love and violence like you can't imagine. I promise I'm not trying to hide it from you. If I were, I wouldn't read it when you were around and would keep it put away." Celeste rubbed her thumb over the spine of the old book, and the wind chimes tinkled outside the kitchen window as the breeze blew through them.

How could she be so patient with me?

"One day, you can read it when I think you're ready. It is a very long tale, longer than any story you have ever read before."

Her description intrigued me and only made me more interested in it. I doubt the book was as great as she made it out to be, though. And why would it take so long to read? It didn't look like that big of a book to me, not any larger than *Gone with the Wind*, and I read that in a week!

"Let's get your stuff, Andie. It's time to go to school. I know it'll be a great day for you. I imagine you will meet all kinds of interesting students and enjoy your classes. Just remember, your day will be what YOU make it. Let nothing or no one get you down." She gave me the pep talk like she'd done this before.

I rolled my eyes at her back after she turned away to walk out the door and trudged out behind her.

Chapter Four

C eleste dropped me off in front of the high school building, full of good wishes and a cheerfulness I wish I felt. I watched all the other students hustling in as I walked up to the big red doors. To my relief, most of them were dressed like me, wearing jeans and old T-shirts, some with hoodies. No one walking into the school wore the latest fashion, and that gave me a little more courage, but I still ducked my head when a guy opened the door for me with a smile. Muttering my thanks, I shuffled into the small hallway only to trip over my own feet and stumble forward.

Ugh, so embarrassing!

I knew my face must be bright red. Steeling myself, I looked up to see if anyone noticed the clumsy new girl. No one around was looking, but as Teagan leaned against the wall by the office door, I realized he had. He smiled with a lopsided grin, arms crossed in front of him as he gazed at me.

Trying to make light of my embarrassment and shake it off, I walked up to him, hoping I could act more confident than I was.

"I had to make a grand entrance, you know!"

Flipping my braid over my shoulder, I laughed as he peeled himself from the wall in one fluid motion. I hadn't realized how tall he was the other day until I stood beside him now. Next to my five-foot-six frame, he towered over me. He had to be at least six two.

"You don't need any grand entrances, Andie. Don't worry about what anyone thinks about you. You'll be the rainbow among the clouds here." He grinned, amusement dancing in his eyes.

Wow, where did *that* come from? I knew my cheeks flushed once again. His poetic words touched a cold place in my heart, and I felt a crack in my armor start to open. Shyly, I smiled up at him, and to my relief, he brushed my embarrassment aside.

"Are you ready for your first day? It's a good school, and I think you'll enjoy the classes. There are difficulties, but overall, it's a great place to be." He reached forward, grabbing the backpack off my shoulder, casually slinging it over his as if it weighed next to nothing. Stunned by this gesture, I stared. He seemed to think nothing of it and turned to head down the hall.

Chivalry wasn't dead!

"Follow me, Andie. I know your schedule, so I'll show you where your first class is. Mr. Sloan's science class. I'm going to warn you: don't ask about dissecting frogs. You'll be in for a huge speech about how inhumane it is." I followed close on his heels, trying to figure out why the teacher would consider dissecting frogs inhumane. You know, because they were already dead?

"Uh, okay. That's a little weird. But I guess there are worse things. He sounds like an interesting person," I offered.

Teagan opened the door, holding it for me as he swept his hand in toward the room, before handing my backpack back. As I brushed by him, he leaned in to whisper, "You'll meet a lot of interesting people here, Andie. See you after first period. Try not to cause too much trouble."

I turned around to look at him, but he had already left.

Finding an empty desk near the back of the classroom, I sat down, placing my backpack by my feet. Several kids around me smiled, and some even said hi before class started. As Mr. Sloan welcomed everyone, the hairs on the back of my neck prickled. I felt someone watching me.

Scanning the room, everyone faced forward, all except one guy. He sat near the corner in the back row, his feet kicked out in front of him, arms crossed tight against his chest, and his steely stare directed at me. If I described the look on his face, it would be menacing. But that was absurd. Why would this guy have any reason to look at me with such hate? He sneered at me before I frowned back, turning my head to Mr. Sloan as he welcomed me to Junction High.

The teacher went through roll call, and I found out who the jerk in the corner was. I wouldn't forget his name anytime soon after the way he had reacted to me. *Hunter Thorn*. Seemed fitting, since the look he had given me was that of a hunter staring down his prey. His piercing brown eyes had caused goosebumps to pimple my skin and a shiver to run down my spine. As the teacher lectured on molecules, I tried my best to ignore Hunter, but it was impossible. Periodically, I felt his gaze. Each time caused another round of goosebumps to travel over my skin.

The bell finally rang after what seemed like forever, and I met Teagan as he came down the hall. Hunter was long forgotten at the warmth of Teagan's smile. He had such a genuine way about him that made me feel comfortable.

He asked how my class had been before his smile turned into a grimace as he looked over my shoulder. I looked to see what had caused his demeanor to suddenly change. And wouldn't you know it, Hunter stood by the classroom door with a similar expression directed at Teagan. For a few seconds, it appeared as if they were in the midst of a stare-off, communicating silently with one another as only men can. Hunter broke the stare first, with a smirk that didn't quite reach his stony eyes as his gaze slid over me. Turning, he ambled off, whistling as he went.

"Hang out here for a minute, Andie. I'll be right back," Teagan said, his voice strained. He squeezed my shoulder as he followed in Hunter's direction.

He called out to Hunter, who turned around defensively, as if expecting Teagan to attack him. His forehead creased with agitation, and he gave Teagan that same menacing stare he had given me in the classroom. Tension rolled off the two of them as they spoke in low tones. Hunter shook his head and appeared to be even more agitated by what Teagan said. Responding, he pointed at me, his finger jabbing the air as his eyes met mine, nostrils flaring before he turned and stormed off.

I didn't know what to make of the encounter between the two guys. It was confusing, if a little intriguing. Something about me set Hunter off, and from the way Teagan responded, he knew why.

"Teagan, what happened? He gives me the creeps," I whispered, my spine tingling as we turned to walk to our next period. He ran his hand through his hair and sighed.

"Hunter is... different. No one can figure him out. He doesn't talk much to any of us and has kept to himself since he started here last year. He gives off a bad vibe and always seems angry at the world. The best thing to do is to keep your distance from him."

He said this so firmly I wondered if he knew more than he said. Their exchange had been heated, but afraid to tick Teagan off with more questions, I stayed quiet. I knew I'd have plenty of time to figure it out. But for now, I had to get through this stupid day.

At 3:30, the bell rang, and I was beyond ready to go home. Celeste was right about the classes and teachers. I had enjoyed them all. Well, except for science. I had been so focused on ignoring Hunter that I wasn't able to pay attention. My sociology class seemed the most promising. Mrs. Tully, or Cherri—she wanted her students to call her by her first name instead—was down to earth, and she was excited about what she taught. Her quirky personality and enthusiasm rubbed off on all the students, including me.

Celeste sat in the car, waiting for me. I was so ready to get my driver's license and be able to drive myself everywhere. It was embarrassing to be a junior in high school and still have to have someone pick me up. I would look for a part-time job once I get my license and save up money to buy a car. I hated having to rely on anyone.

As I walked closer to the car, it looked as if Celeste was talking to someone. There were a lot of times I walked in on her talking, but there was never anyone else there. Between Anne, Celeste, and Charlie, I sometimes felt like I was losing my mind.

She turned around to the backseat and continued as if she were carrying on a conversation with someone sitting back there. I strained to see if there was anyone else, but there was no one. Spotting me as I got closer, she waved, not worried at all about how weird it was that she sat there chatting away with absolutely no one.

Sighing, I got into the car.

After we got home, I made a sandwich and decided to sit out on the back patio to do my homework. The weather was warmer today, the sun shone high in the sky, and I planned to enjoy the warmth while I could. Charlie squawked in the sunroom as he watched me through the window. I couldn't tell what he was saying this time, but he stared right at me with his big round bird eyes. Sticking my tongue out at him, I turned back to finish the last question on my ethics homework.

Done! I closed the notebook and set it aside. I was about to kick back and put my feet up when I noticed movement out of the corner of my eye and swung my head around to look.

It was that darn kid standing by the tree line again!

He wore brown shorts, a short-sleeved white button-up, and suspenders attached to the shorts. White socks were pulled up to his calves, and his shoes were weird-looking loafers. *Who wore clothes like that?* I wondered if he was homeless. Something was tucked under his arm, but from this distance, I couldn't make out what it was.

I wanted to find out who he was and what he was doing out here by himself, so I motioned for him to come over. He laughed, and the sound carried over the breeze. Shaking his head at me, he pointed to the woods and then turned to walk back into them.

That little stinker!

"No! Wait!" I yelled, jumping out of my chair to run after him. I was determined to find out who this kid was, and I only made it halfway across the yard before he disappeared into the thick trees. Reaching the edge of the forest, the crunching of his footsteps echoed as he traveled further away from me. I stopped and looked back at the house, knowing I should tell Celeste before going after him, but I would never catch up or find him if I took the time. So, pushing back branches, I followed the faint sound of leaves crackling underfoot. A giggle drifted in the air every now and then as I traveled deeper into the brush.

The air was much colder here, and I shivered. The light couldn't break through the dense cover of the trees, making the forest dark and dreary. Noise from bugs scurrying around and the cacophony of birds high in the branches somehow soothed my sense of unease as I made my way closer to where I thought the last giggle had come from.

After ten minutes of walking, with no idea of where I was going, a clearing appeared ahead. Pushing through the weeds and sticks that surrounded it, I saw that the brambles all around the edge formed a natural fence. The clearing was large, with green clover covering the ground in a thick blanket. To my right, a small stream trickled, and an enormous oak tree towered in the back, making the surrounding trees seem tiny in comparison. It reminded me of redwoods I had seen in pictures. *It was huge*! I couldn't imagine how old the tree was. It had to have been here forever.

At that moment, the sneaky little kid showed himself, skipping out from behind the big oak and waving at me before continuing to skip around it again.

"Hey kid, what are you doing out here?" I yelled at him. "Where are your parents? Are they somewhere around here? What's your name?"

He didn't answer but stopped his constant skipping, which, let me tell you, was getting on my nerves. Tired of yelling across the clearing at him, I moved closer. His impish smile made dimples in either cheek appear, and he still had something tucked under his arm. After taking a closer look, I realized it was a book bound in leather. Patting it gently, he put his forefinger to his lips.

Was he telling me to be quiet? Forget that! No way would I leave him out here by himself.

"Come on, kid, tell me your name and we'll go find your parents. Not much longer until it gets dark. You can't be out here by yourself."

He jumped away as I again moved even closer, running around the back of the oak where I couldn't see him. Sighing in frustration, I took off after him again.

"I've had my fill of this game now," I muttered to myself. Rounding the back of the tree, my knee hit something and I went flying forward, hitting the ground *hard*.

I rolled over, groaning as I stared up at the tree canopy. There were sparkling lights in the thick branches and leaves, blinking in and out, dancing around and through them. I must have hit my head really hard.

Gingerly, I touched my forehead, and my hand came away sticky with blood. *Gah! How clumsy!* I really hoped the wound wouldn't need stitches.

I cursed the little kid that seemed to enjoy playing this game. Where did he go anyway? How did he disappear into thin air? Breathing slowly to calm myself, I turned to the oak tree, studying the dark bark looming in front of my face. I studied the thick trunk; rough lines in the bark looked as if something had scored the wood years ago. One of the lines ran up to a knobby looking growth, and above that,

I noticed a light. Looking back up at the canopy of branches, no light shined through, and I shivered.

Pain shot through my head as I sat up too fast, and I grabbed ahold of a gigantic root that must have been what I tripped over. Pushing myself to stand, I kept my eyes trained on the strange light in the trunk. It was only about as big around as my fingertip. Bending closer, I placed my hands on the rough bark and saw that the warm light spilled out from a hole in the tree.

What the heck?

Leaning close, I peered through it.

Gasping, I backed away. *Okay… I must have hit my head really hard, and right now I'm knocked out, and this is all a dream*, I rationalized. There was no way what I saw through that hole could be real! Rubbing my eyes, I held my breath and looked through it again.

Inside, a huge library spanned so many floors high I couldn't even see them all. Books lined the walls, and a winding staircase twisted and turned up to each story. There were trinkets and artifacts piled on tables and the floor, and all manner of plants and small trees grew willy-nilly throughout the large room. Against the far wall, a fireplace crackled, surrounded by several armchairs and more of those twinkling lights that had been in the branches were scattered throughout the plants. They reminded me of lightning bugs blinking off and on.

It. Was. Magical.

Just then, something streaked through my line of vision, startling me. Was that a dragonfly? Iridescent wings fluttered, and it was about the same size as one.

Determined to figure out what was going on, I ran my hands around the bark where the light came from, trying to find a way in. The knobby growth resembled a doorknob, and the hole sat right above it.

Was it a keyhole?

Then it hit me. I couldn't believe I hadn't thought of the small key! I had put it on a ribbon and worn it around my neck with the hope that

I could give it back to the boy should I ever see him again. Pulling it out from under my shirt, I lifted it over my head, staring at the small key. It was the perfect size, and something inside of me knew it would fit.

Excited but nervous all at once, I put the key in the opening, turning it gently. A strange clicking noise began, and a tinkling of bells sounded as a door creaked open in the wood. Heat escaped and flowed over me. Overwhelmed, I tried to take in everything as I stood in the doorway looking in.

"Don't ya stand there with ta door open. Come in, come in!" a rough voice said, and I yelped in surprise.

Putting my hand to my heart in shock, I searched the room, wide-eyed, trying to see who had spoken.

"Shut ta door! You don't want ta Fomorians to get in. We can't be having that," the voice said, louder this time.

Confused about what Fomorians were, and where the voice originated from, I quickly stepped inside and closed the door behind me. The clicking and tinkling sounded again, and I turned to look at the door to see that the inside had gears with bells hanging from them. What an odd locking mechanism.

Beside the door was a rug with shoes laid out on it. Some were sneakers, some old loafers, and a pair of weird-looking boots with pointy toes and cuffs at the ankles.

"Mmhmm..."

The voice cleared its throat behind me as I studied the shoes. Whirling around, a figure as tall as my knees had come out from behind one of the large tropical plants growing from the ground in a corner. As it walked closer, I could see a little man-shaped creature with large pointed ears, a long bulbous nose, and leathery brown skin. He wore an oversized brown shirt belted with leather at the waist. Skinny legs stuck out from underneath with bare feet too large for his body. On top of his head, he wore a little red stocking cap that reminded me of what the kids wore in *The Night Before Christmas*. As he stood in front of me, my mouth moved, but no words came out. His eyes were big, larger than any human's, dark, with pupils that took up most of his eyes.

He peered at me in silence for a while, looking me up and down before stating, "You'll do."

Turning, he grabbed ahold of my hand, pulling me to where chairs were situated in front of the warm fire. My mouth was dry, still not able to form words. This man... *thing* looked like what I imagined an elf would look like. *He could not be human*! I let him lead me to the sitting area where he sat me down in a comfortable chair, the fire warming me as it blazed and crackled.

Once again, he stood in front of me. This time, we were at eye level.

"Name's Balwyn. We have been waiting for ya to arrive for a long time. Don't know what took ya so long." He scowled at me, his hairy eyebrows hanging low over his large eyes.

I was baffled and in shock.

"Um. Balwyn... I don't understand what you're talking about. Who's 'we?' And why have you been waiting for a long time for me?"

He scowled again and shook his head as he turned away, muttering to himself before walking toward the large plant he had come from, disappearing from sight. The little lights scattered in his wake.

"He's right. We have been waiting a long time for you," an amused voice whispered into my ear. I jumped, frightened to find what creature was behind me this time.

A low buzzing sounded in my ear, and then something zipped right by my face, circling my head so fast I couldn't keep up.

"Please stop. You're making me dizzy," I complained.

At that moment, Balwyn came back out from hiding, carrying a tray that held a steaming mug. It smelled like hot cocoa.

"Eira! Quit yer flyin' round ta girls head. We have gots to talk to her quick like before we run out of time!" He scowled at the creature buzzing above my head. I watched as it dove onto the chair beside me, doing a somersault only to land back on its tiny toes like a ballet dancer.

My mouth dropped open. By now, after being in this magical tree and meeting Balwyn, you would think nothing could surprise me. Never in my life had I seen or imagined the creatures in front of me existed. Only in the fairy tales I grew up reading, or in Disney movies.

Still striking a pose, the little creature had its arms in the air, one toe pointed out, posing as if waiting for applause. Not really knowing what to do, I clapped, and the creature jumped and then curtsied. *It actually curtsied*! While the tiny thing preened for my attention, Balwyn handed me the cup.

"Drink up, girlie. Ya need ta warm up and calm down."

I blew on the warm drink, and tiny little white things that I hoped were marshmallows floated on the top. It had to be cocoa.

Glancing over at the small creature who waited on my attention, I decided that this had to be an actual fairy. Sitting on the arm of the chair, the tiny creature studied me while resting its chin in its tiny porcelain hands. It wore a little skirt and top made from flower petals, all different hues of pink and purple intertwined with each other. The wings that extended out behind it were iridescent like a dragonfly. Silver hair was arranged in a mass of braids atop its head. It had to be a girl fairy.

She must have been what I saw fly by so fast when I looked through the keyhole! She blinked her green eyes at me, and her mouth formed a tiny, beautiful smile as I studied her. As if she couldn't hide her excitement for more than a minute, her patience gone, she clapped her hands, and I noticed her skin appeared luminous, almost pearlescent.

"Andie, right?" she asked me in her squeaky little voice. I nodded. "I'm Eira, and I am so excited to meet you. You likely could already tell that I'm Fae. Or you might be more familiar with the term 'fairy.' Balwyn is a Brownie, and we are the keepers of this Mighty Oak." She swung her arms out wide. "We've waited many years for you, Andie. You will save our world from the darkness and destruction that is coming."

Well, that's ridiculous.

Why in the world would they think I would be able to save anything? I'm just a teenager—I can't even drive! My mind spun, and I wasn't sure what to say, so I sipped the cocoa, hoping it would take away the chill and give me time to think. It was delicious and creamy, warming my body from my belly to my toes. Relaxing into the chair, I sighed, and Eira and Balwyn watched in silence.

Eira hopped from the chair to perch on my arm, and then placed her tiny hand on top of mine. "Andie, I know this is a lot to take in, but you must listen to me. Your mother, as hard as this may be to believe, was one of us. So was your grandmother. Your mother died trying to find the Keys, hoping to spare you from your fate. But she wasn't the one meant to find them. She was not who had been foreseen to save us all. There are four Keys you must find. We need each one to keep our worlds from burning, and the evilness that surrounds us from taking over," she said softly, fear clear in her eyes.

"I can't explain all the details to you right now, but before long more will be revealed. You must go home now. Your Guardian is waiting for you. Come back tomorrow, and we will discuss this further to prepare you for what is coming." Done with her ominous speech, she flew off to one of the flowering plants growing over the balcony above us, rich with purple flowers cascading over the rail.

Balwyn took the mug from me in one hand and extended his other to help me up. "Come now, Miss Andie. Time ta go!"

Everything had my head spinning. The questions that I had for them flew around my brain in such a maelstrom that I wasn't able to form them and get them out.

Balwyn led me over to the door faster than seemed possible, as if he knew I had questions and wanted me out before I could ask them. Grasping my hand in his warm, rough one, he looked up at me pointing to the rug littered with different shoes. "Next time, ya need to take your footwear off when you enter."

Who really cared about shoes at a time like this? Not knowing him well enough to tempt ticking him off, I kept my mouth shut, tipping my head once at him. He leaned forward, whispering a word I couldn't hear, and the door started the strange clicking and tinkling noise and slung back open again. Balwyn shooed me out the door.

"Out ya go. Can't let them get in! Remember ta come back tamorrow!" he yelled, shutting the door behind me.

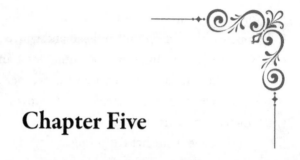

Chapter Five

Nighttime had fallen, and the moon lit the forest floor. I felt absolutely stunned. The air had turned cold and crisp, and I shivered after being in the tree's warmth. Wrapping my arms around myself, I glanced back to see the light gone from the keyhole. There was absolutely no sign that a door was ever there.

Hurrying through the woods, I thought about everything I'd been told and all that I'd seen. What happened to the kid I had been following? Where did he disappear to? He had to be a part of all of this as well. It was obvious to me now that he had dropped the key to the door, knowing I would find it. He led me to the tree with a purpose.

He must have been what they called "Fae." Some sort of fairy, but what kind? And my mother, Nan and I all shared their blood? That meant I was Fae too. How was that possible? My head swam with all this new information, and I wasn't sure how to process everything. It was all too overwhelming.

As I hurried out of the woods and onto the back lawn, Celeste relaxed on the patio with a small fire going in the pit, her usual mug of hot tea steaming beside her. I approached at a snail's pace, my mind racing to figure out what to tell her I had been doing for so long. There was *no* way she would believe me if I told her the truth.

"Hey, Celeste, I'm sorry I'm so late getting in—and that I didn't tell you where I was going. When I was in the woods, I tripped over a tree root and hit my head. I must have been knocked out for a while."

Sort of the truth, except the part about being knocked out. I carefully touched the cut on my forehead and winced a little. It really was sore. Celeste said nothing, but her smug look and her signature eyebrow raise told me she didn't entirely believe me.

"Child, you need not deceive me. I know every minute detail of your whereabouts this evening."

I protested, but she held up a finger, closed her eyes, and shook her head, her mouth firm. "No, Andie, I do. I read you the moment you walked out of the woods. I saw your thoughts as your mind raced to figure out what to tell me. I viewed everything as if through your eyes, dear."

Again, I was at a loss. Every time I turned around, there was something so incredible that my mind could barely keep up. I sat down hard on the stones of the patio, not bothering to sit in a chair. The events of the night wore me out, and I felt the stress building.

The scrape of a chair on the patio sounded behind me, and I took a deep breath of the flower-scented air. Celeste gently placed a blanket around my shoulders. If she could read my mind, then she knew how chilled I felt.

Oh, God! She can read my mind!

Furiously, I tried to think back, wondering if I had thought of anything that would seriously be embarrassing for her to know. She sat crosslegged on the stone in front of me, tucking her long skirt under her knees as I stared hard at the ground. Placing her finger under my chin, she lifted my face.

"Andie, I haven't been reading your mind all this time. Only when I worry you might be in danger, and just now, to make sure you learned what you were meant to. Don't be afraid of all this new information. I know it's a lot to take in. All your understanding will come in time. Now it's time for me to be honest."

She stared into my eyes, and I gulped because I wasn't sure I wanted to know more, or if I could handle more.

"But you must, and you can. I promise you, Andie, you are strong, stronger than you can imagine," she responded to the question in my mind.

"Your nan and I met in these woods. Things were so different then. They were full of all kinds of Fae. We lived there, you see, enjoying the vast and secluded area where we could be ourselves in plain sight. We ran with the wind in our hair, climbed the tallest trees to look out at the strange world around us in awe."

Her eyes glittered with unshed tears, brighter than they had been before. Her sadness was overwhelming. Taking a deep breath and wiping her eyes, she continued.

"Then one day, a group entered the woods, hunting us. We had never seen nor heard of these creatures before, but oh, we would never forget them after that day. They slaughtered many of our friends and family, showing no mercy, not even for the young. They were cruel, vile creatures. I hid from them in the brush when your nan scurried under with me. No one noticed her movements. We both listened as the leader told the rest of their group to look for the ones with gray eyes."

I looked up at Celeste, and she nodded. She knew exactly what I thought without having to read my mind. Nan's eyes had been a bright, steely gray, like mine. I always thought my eyes were rather dull, but Nan's always seemed to be a bright and beautiful silvery gray. I remembered when I was little, telling her they looked like the hematite rocks we found once on a hike. Brighter when she was happy, turning to a darker shade when she was upset.

"I don't understand what our eye color has to do with anything, Celeste. Does it have something to do with our family in particular?"

"You come from a mighty race of Fae. Your people all have the same gray eyes. We won't go into all of that right now, though. You will learn about the past and all that it holds soon. And that past is not as important as your future, and the rest of ours. You will do hard things, but they will lead to great things. You are our hope."

Squeezing my leg, she stood up and stretched. Her arms reached for the sky, her long silver braid hanging behind her, the moon a bright orb above her head. It almost appeared as if she cupped the moon, and it reminded me of a famous painting of the Moon Goddess Diana. Unraveling from her stretch, Celeste tipped her head to me with a Cheshire smile.

Wait. What!?

I started to ask her, but she cut me off, effectively turning the conversation. "Come, dear, you've got a long day ahead of you. Say, how is school going? That young man we met the other day seemed nice," she said as we walked into the house.

Why did she even ask me? Obviously, she could read my mind if she wanted to.

"Teagan is a nice guy. He's helped me a lot, and I think we'll be pretty good friends. I haven't gotten to meet many other people yet. There is this one guy, though, Hunter. He's so strange. He instantly hated me, and I can't figure out why. Teagan didn't seem to like him very much either. The school itself is okay, I guess," I said, not wanting to be too optimistic.

"Well, I think you ought to invite Teagan over for a little while after school, and anyone else you'd like. It would do you good to spend time with someone your age. I can grill burgers for dinner, and the weather will be so nice. You can eat outside or have a picnic! What do you think, Andie?" she asked excitedly as if it was the best idea since sliced bread.

"I don't know if he'd want to come over Celeste. But sure, I'll invite him. Just make sure Charlie doesn't say anything inappropriate." I laughed as I went up the stairs to bed.

"Andie?"

I stopped and turned around.

"Don't forget your music tonight. You don't want to tempt the nightmares..."

I wasn't surprised at all that she knows about those too. The way she said it sounded almost ominous, causing a shiver to run up my spine and the hair on my arms to stand up.

No... I didn't want to tempt the nightmares.

I settled in bed for the night, reading another book I found in Celeste's library. It was intriguing, and I had a hard time putting the story down. When I got to an intense part of the book, a noise from the backyard startled me so much that I almost fell out of the bed. It hadn't been loud, but I was so focused on who killed Mrs. Brisby that I tuned out everything around me. The slight noise sounded again, and then I heard whispers.

Quiet as a mouse, I slid out of bed and tiptoed to the window. Pulling back the curtain just enough to see, I peered down at the yard. There were four figures hunched together, all dressed in blue robes.

What are they doing?

As if they heard my thought, all four heads turned to look up at me. Celeste, Anne, and Sari. The fourth person kept their face averted, but a blonde ponytail poked out from the blue hood. I let the curtain drop, belatedly realizing that it didn't matter since they had seen me already. They weren't chanting or dancing in circles, so I suspected that they were just visiting and being weird old women. My imagination already cooked up all kinds of scenarios. I was seriously too tired to worry about what those women were doing.

Crawling back into bed, I switched off the light and turned my music on. It wasn't long before sleep pulled me under.

Chapter Six

The next day at school flew by, and luckily, I didn't run into Hunter at all. I also made another friend, Presley. She was the total opposite of me: blonde hair, blue eyes, and much more feminine in her fashion tastes. She had approached me in the library during our homeroom period, plopped herself down in the chair in front of me, and we struck up a conversation about our favorite books. It blew me away that she enjoyed fantasy books as much as I did.

Despite her looks, she seemed brilliant and kind. We immediately hit it off, and I was embarrassed that I had stereotyped her. I had to work on that. Come to find out, she was also a friend of Teagan. She had grown up down the street from him and told me a few funny stories. I would have to tease him about them later.

Remembering what Celeste had said about inviting Teagan for dinner, I shyly asked them if they would like to come. To my surprise, both said yes, so we made plans to meet there after school. I was excited to get to know them better, to maybe have a chance to actually have close friends. I'd never been interested in building relationships with other kids my age before, and it was a strange but exhilarating feeling.

That afternoon, as I sat with Charlie trying to teach him how to say "wowza," someone pulled in the drive.

"Hey, Charlie, I've got some new friends for you to meet!" I hollered at him as I rushed outside.

"New friends! New friends!" he sang.

I ran to the front door and flung it wide open. But it wasn't Teagan and Presley standing on the doorstep. It was Hunter. Both of his hands were shoved into the pockets of his jeans, his dark hair hanging over one eye with a mischievous grin on his face. My mind raced to figure out what he wanted, and my excitement faded, replaced with tension and wariness. How did he even figure out where I lived?

A sleek black and chrome motorcycle sat parked out by the road. Figured. A motorcycle would be something he would drive. Dark and dangerous.

"Uh, hi, Hunter. Did you come here to try to scare me away again?"

I was abrupt and blunt with him because I wasn't about to give this guy the satisfaction of being rude to me again. Nan always taught me to know my worth, and I knew I didn't have to put up with any crap from him again. I could give it back just as well as I could take it.

He shrugged, the smile on his face slipping, and his eyes turned stormy. The change in emotion was unexpected and familiar. I recognized my own attitude in him. Trying to be tough to cover up emotions that we thought would make us seem weak.

And just as quickly, that show of emotion disappeared, the mischievous look appearing again in his eyes, and with raised eyebrows, he leaned forward, tugging on my hair.

Swatting at his hand, I ground out, "Quit! Tell me what you want before I slam this door in your face."

His face fell once again as he took a step back, putting distance between the two of us

"Listen, I didn't come here to scare you or tell you to leave town. I didn't come here intending to make you mad. I'm not very good at this. I came to apologize, but if you'd rather I didn't, I'll leave..." he trailed off, turning to go.

"Wait, what?" I stuttered. He turned around slowly, a resigned look on his face.

"Why would you suddenly feel bad about how you treated me the day we met? You obviously have something against me. It's hard for me to believe you had a change of heart since I didn't do anything in the first place."

I put my hands on my hips, waiting on what lie he might come up with now. He seemed like the kind of guy who lied a lot.

"Andie, I thought you were something you aren't. I'm sorry—really, I am. I'm not an easy guy to get along with, and when I think someone is a threat, I have a hard time curbing my instincts. I know you don't understand, but I had to come and apologize," Hunter stated plainly. He seemed sincere, and I reluctantly sensed that he told the truth.

"Well, I guess only time will tell who the real Hunter is. If you can prove you're not that mean jerk from the first day of school, I might consider your apology," I stated.

"Ohhhh... You'll *consider*, huh?" His eyes sparkled again, and I knew he was amused. Turning to walk back to his motorcycle, he spoke over his shoulder, voice dripping with arrogance. "You'll accept. I know you will."

He slipped his helmet on as another vehicle barreled up the driveway. Dust from the white rock flew in the air behind the black truck before it came to an abrupt stop behind Hunters motorcycle. Teagan and Presley hopped out, and the looks on their faces as they stared at Hunter were priceless. Presley's mouth hung open wide, and Teagan was furious. Uh-oh...

"Teagan, Presley," Hunter acknowledged them.

They both stood there, still as statues, staring at him. Teagan showed open animosity, while Presley looked a bit star struck. Hunter glanced back at me once before sliding smoothly onto his bike. As he turned the ignition on, the bike let out a roar made louder by him revving it up. Giving us a salute, he drove off, kicking up dust behind his tires as we watched until we couldn't see him any longer.

"What the heck was he doing here, Andie?" Teagan asked as we walked up to the porch. A frown creased his eyebrows, and I could tell he was really worked up about it.

"Well, he basically told me that he was sorry for the way he treated me when we first met. I'm not sure why, but I believe him. I wanted to slam the door in his face when I first saw him, but something about the way he acted made me think that this tough act is just that: an act. I kind of felt sorry for him, guys."

Teagan rolled his eyes but calmed down some. He was trying hard not to say what was on his mind.

"What, Teagan? What has you so wound up about him being here? I don't understand what the deal is between you two. If I didn't know any better, I would guess you thought he was some evil villain," I joked, attempting to lighten the mood.

"He's hot in a kind of evil villain sort of way," Presley said with sass, looking at Teagan from the side of her eye. She was trying to work Teagan up even more, and the look of shock he gave her was amusing.

I laughed, and she joined me, but Teagan didn't seem to find her funny at all. I agreed with Presley, though. Maybe it was the mystery surrounding him or the bad boy vibe he embodied. Something drew me to him regardless of how he acted.

Rather than staying out here talking about Hunter and letting Teagan get worked up more than he already was, I steered them toward the house. "Oh, you've got to meet chatty Charlie! He's been waiting to meet you both, Celeste too! She's around here somewhere."

Chapter Seven

While I lay in bed, I thought about the fun evening we all had together. Celeste was so excited to meet Teagan and Presley, and Charlie wouldn't shut up. I thought Presley would never stop laughing when he shouted "wowza" at her. Talk about hilarious! Teagan had helped Celeste grill the burgers, and then we all sat outside on the patio enjoying each other's company. It just felt comfortable and right.

Presley informed me I just *had* to go to Moonlight and Magic. I remembered seeing the sign on the office door and asked her to tell me about it. She had said it was a dance where everyone dressed up as a mythical creature, sort of like a costume party with a theme. Ironic, but I agreed it sounded fun. If only I weren't off doing whatever Eira and Balwyn thought I needed to do to save the world. Sighing, I flipped on my music and turned out the light.

As I drifted off to sleep, my brain screamed at me and I jolted up in bed.

Oh, crap! I had forgotten to go to the tree!

Sitting straight up, I flung off the covers and tore the earbuds out of my ears, scrambling up, I threw on some clothes. Balwyn and Eira would be so disappointed in me if I didn't show up as I promised. I couldn't let them down. Grabbing a flashlight, I slapped on my beanie and left the house.

The night was darker than usual, the moon hidden behind heavy clouds. Coyotes howled in the distance, and the air was chilly. Thank goodness I had the foresight to put on my hoodie. Hurrying, I flicked the flashlight on as I entered the woods, hoping I didn't have an issue finding the tree again. Leaves and pine needles crunched under my feet; the smell of damp earth tickled my nose. Five minutes into my walk, little lights flitted in and out through the trees ahead of me, lining up, illuminating a path, and showing me the way.

As I got closer, I realized the lights came from hundreds of fairies. The number of them made me stop and stare in sheer amazement. One sat on a low branch close to me, and I bent down to study it. A smile lit the tiny coffee-colored face, and a small orb glowed from the belt around its waist. I wondered what they made the spheres from. Standing back up, I glanced around, and all the fairies were waving and smiling, excited and happy. Each fairy looked like a miniature human with wings.

Catching myself staring, I remembered the task at hand and resumed walking. They all fell in line behind me as I followed the bouncing lights from the ones stationed in front of me. The tree loomed enormous, this time lit up brightly. The dancing lights shone on every branch, and the hum of hundreds of wings fluttered around in excitement. I didn't understand what was happening, but the fairies knew something I didn't. My heart raced as I wondered what they had in store for me.

The group of fairies in front of me parted, making an opening, so I could walk to the tree. I halted in my tracks when I saw who sat against it, confused. Why was Anne here? At least I thought it was Anne.

She wore a long violet gossamer gown, flowers twined through a crown on her head, and fairies flew around her face, stopping to kiss her cheeks every few seconds. Lifting a hand, she motioned for me to come closer.

"Anne? What's going on?" I asked, my voice trembling, and my stomach felt as if butterflies were flying around erratically in it. I couldn't wrap my mind around why she would be here.

"Andie, there is so much for you to learn." She chuckled, and the fairies joined her merriment. Their laughter was like the tinkling of a million little bells. "Everything that has happened, and almost everyone you met recently has been for a reason, all leading you to this moment."

Throwing her arms wide, she motioned to the tree and the fairies before continuing. "My real name is Aine, Queen of Fairy. I was sent to keep you safe on your way to Celeste. She knew I could use my gift of persuasion, and my fairies could scout ahead, looking out for any danger to you."

I remembered her talking to her purse on the drive down, and it hit me that she must have had fairies inside of it. So she wasn't crazy after all! I snorted and shook my head, wondering who else I would discover wasn't really who they said they were.

Aine tugged my hand, pulling me down to sit beside her as I gazed at a little fairy bouncing on one of her curls. Up and down, and she didn't notice or care.

"Listen close, Andie, because in a short time your whole life will change. You may seem like a teenage girl right now, but there is a war coming, and you will save us all."

She held up her hand to hush me as I attempted to interrupt. Instantly, I clamped my mouth shut, biting my tongue to hold back the words I wanted to say. Inside my mind, I screamed them anyway. How could I save everyone?! I didn't even understand what I was supposed to be protecting them from!

"There are many creatures you never could imagine are real. So many of the books you read, whether they were about fairies, werewolves, trolls, banshees, or more, are very real creatures. Many of these groups are on our side. But one group, the Fomorians, or Fomori for short, are trying to persuade some stronger packs to join with them to crush us all. Your human world, as well. I can see you do not understand what the Fomori are, correct?" she questioned me.

"No. I don't understand who or what the Fomori are except for what Celeste has told me."

"Fomori are beings that came from the sea and underground to run amok and cause havoc in our worlds. They are the personification of chaos, darkness, and death. At one time, there were a few that broke away from the larger group, who joined and married some Tuatha De Danann, or Fae. That gave many other Fomori reasons to hate us more. Many years ago, during a bloody battle, we defeated them after they had oppressed our people for so long. We lived once again in harmony, and they retreated to the sea and underground. Until they came back, charging into the woods and began searching for your family. The ruler of the Fomori had learned your family descended from Nemed, a gray-eyed warrior king who had won many battles against the Fomori. Every descendant in your family has had gray eyes like yours.

"When Nemed and his people settled in Ireland, they brought four magical treasures with them. Each one from the four cities they hailed from. The treasures are Dagda's Cauldron, the Spear of Lugh, The Stone of Fal, and the Sword of Light. The ruler of the Fomori knew this and coveted them more than anything in this world or the next. He thought if he could only gain these four treasures, he could rule the world and rid it of all he hated. Especially the Tuatha De Danann.

"Traveling many miles to where our people had fled, he captured some of your ancestors and killed them when they wouldn't disclose the whereabouts of the treasure. But one escaped: your grandmother. Celeste helped her. She would not have managed had she not been as strong as she was. She mentioned earlier tonight that she heard your thoughts about the painting of the Goddess Diana. Well, Andie, you're living with the real-life Diana. She is the Goddess of the hunt, the Moon, and nature. To hide your nan safely until they were out of the woods, she called upon all the magic that she could. She called to the animals, to the water nymphs, and the moon to hide their flight far away from there."

Aine sighed, reaching for a leaf beside her that held delicate dew-drops on it. She lifted it, studying it, and then touched the drop, which expanded to fill the whole leaf. Tipping it to her mouth, she drank.

All the information she had given me swirled in my brain, so much now made sense to me. One fairy played with my hair, braiding it gently. In my haste to leave the house, I had left it down. The featherlike touch of the fairy soothed me, and my shoulders relaxed as I realized Aine was not yet finished with her tale.

She turned to look at me, her eyes serious, as she put her hand to my cheek.

"Your Nan hid for many years. She hid who she was from your grandfather. He had no idea. She had your mother who, until she was your age, had no idea either. That's when your nan told her about her heritage and where she came from. Your mother thought she could find the four treasures or, 'Keys' as we like to call them. Despite your nan's warning, she was determined to save us. In her travels, she met your father. A handsome man, different from anyone she had ever been around before. He was not Fae, no, not Fae at all. She became immediately taken with him, and that he could help her with her journey only sweetened the deal."

I sat up straight.

"But if he isn't Fae, then what is he? And, where is he?"

I wanted to hear more about this mystery man Nan had refused to tell me about. Who I had given little thought to throughout my childhood. I had just accepted that he had left. I figured he didn't want me; therefore, I didn't want him. Though, something in my heart ached to learn more about him. To understand why he left me.

"Shh, sweet girl. Quiet that heart of yours. The emotions are flowing out in waves. We know little, but he loved you. He did not leave on his own accord and would not have left if it wasn't for a good reason. None of us could gain knowledge of his whereabouts either." Aine stroked my hand, trailing her finger over my knuckles.

"Now, where was I? Oh, yes. He was a powerful and talented Warlock, his powers immeasurable. He tried to save your mother from the
Fomori, but something went very wrong. Only he knows, and only he
can tell the tale. But now you understand what you are: part-Fae and
part-Witch. You have no powers right now because, for your entire life,
we all worked hard to suppress them. We couldn't take a chance that
the Fomori would find you. Now, you must go on this quest, and you'll
need all your powers available to you. Since none of us is a Witch, we
cannot tell you what those might be, but, once you enter the other
realm in search of the Keys, your powers will come to the forefront.
Maybe not all at once, and maybe not as soon as we would like, but they
will come. You must use them to your advantage. Your Fae magic will
become available to you as well. They might not be as strong as your
other powers, but they will be needed. Now, time to get started, young
lady."

She stood up, smoothing out her gown, and stared down at me, siz-
ing me up. I had a hard time picturing the old "Anne." Power emanated
from her as she reached out and grasped my hand, turning it over and
pushing up the sleeves of my hoodie to expose my forearm. Resting her
hand over it, a slight tingle began, then a quick flash of heat before cool-
ness took the sharp bite of pain away. When she removed her hand, she
exposed a delicate black symbol on my arm. Intricate and beautiful.

"What is this, Aine?" I looked from my arm into her glowing green
eyes.

"It is an Unalome. It will be a symbol of your journey, before and
after what will come. It shows you the path isn't always straight, perfect,
or even the 'right' direction. Your path to awakening will be filled with
missteps, lessons to learn, and suffering. This is to remind you," she said
with powerful conviction. She leaned over and touched the Unalome
tattoo with her finger, making it glow.

"*Si vis pacem, para bellum*," she said.

At my questioning look, she explained the words were Latin. *If you want peace, prepare for war.* Swallowing hard, I stood a little straighter at the fear of the unknown. I knew that I must do this, even if I didn't think I could.

She continued, "You will search for the four Keys, and you will know what they are when you find this symbol on them, only this symbol." She pointed her finger above us, and a soft light appeared in the air. Using her finger to draw, the light transformed. Four intricate Celtic knots appeared. As she finished the last knot, she explained it was the Quaternary Knot, symbolizing the treasures of Tuatha: the Sword, Cauldron, Stone, and Spear. Staring at the symbol in shock, I turned to Aine again.

"I've seen that before! In a dream after I got here. Something chased me as I ran through the woods. The symbols were on all the trees." My teeth chattered as I realized my dream hadn't really been a dream at all, but a kind of premonition.

"Ahh, you are a Seer then," Aine stated matter-of-factly. "You can see future events yet to take place. This is a mighty gift bestowed upon you, and you must use it wisely. Never forget the things you've seen, and use them to your advantage. But be warned: some visions may seem clear to you but have an entirely different meaning. It is up to you to discern the truth."

So, all this time, my nightmares were visions of things that would happen? Could she frighten me any more? The dreams I had were horrific and frightening, and she was telling me they would come true? Yeah, not sure I wanted anything to do with that.

"Aine, how can I possibly go through those nightmares again? I don't even know how I'm supposed to fight the creatures that are in them and keep them from killing me," I whined. "I don't think I can do this. I'm not who you think I am!"

Aine wrapped her arm around my shoulders, pulling me into her warm side. "Shh, child. You can do more than you think possible.

Soon, you will be more powerful than all of us, and you will cast those demons out of your nightmares. I promise you will not be alone." She smiled down at me, running her hand over my hair soothingly.

"Now, it's time to go. The portal won't wait forever, and you must be on your way to Finias to find the first key."

The doorway creaked open, emitting a soft, warm glow from inside. The outline of Balwyn and Eira as they stood off to the side of the door, waiting, was clear. I looked around uncertainly. Surely someone would stop me, say it was all a joke. But the fairies just smiled in encouragement. Some nodding at me, some waving, a few blowing kisses.

Aine was stoic as she watched me, her eyes bold and confident that I wouldn't fail her. Taking a deep breath, I steeled myself for the unknown. Faking confidence I didn't feel, I nodded at them all and then stepped through the doorway.

A commotion broke out behind me, and I turned back. Eira landed on my shoulder, and Balwyn stood silently beside me. The fairies pointed, turning excitedly to each other as a figure emerged from the woods, crashing through the brambles. Light brown hair glinted in the moonlight as he looked at me from across the clearing. *Teagan!* What was he doing here?

Before I processed it, more crashing came from the opposite side, and another figure emerged directly across from him. Whoever or whatever it was, I couldn't make out more than two glowing eyes in the darkness. The eyes danced closer to us, and Teagan didn't move from his position. He glared at the figure moving ever closer to the light, while the fairies were delighted.

A dark boot stepped into the glow, with the rest of the shadowy figure following to reveal the one and only... *Hunter.* What were they doing here, surrounded by fairies? I watched as they stalked toward each other to meet in the middle of the clearing, eyes locked, hatred oozing from every pore.

Toe-to-toe, they continued their stupid male stare-off as I watched, exasperated and desperate for someone to explain to me what the heck was going on. Why were they here?

Instead of killing each other, as I suspected they wanted to do, they nodded to each other, turning as one to approach Aine, all animosity gone without a trace. Stopping in front of her, they bowed low. The gesture told me they weren't just regular schoolkids.

Oh no. They had to be a part of all of this too.

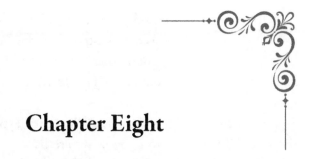

Chapter Eight

"I see you got my summons," Aine said. "I wasn't sure if you would come, knowing you would have to work together, but we need you."

After speaking with Aine quietly, they both looked over at me as I silently stood in the doorway. Teagan's expression was grave and concerned; Hunter's was the total opposite. He was carefree, with a grin on his face as he looked me up and down causing tingles to run over my spine. Smoothly, as one, they strode forward to stand in front of me.

"Andie," Teagan mumbled before he placed his hand over his heart and bowed. The gesture was confusing, but before I had a chance to say anything, Hunter grabbed my hand. Instead of bowing, he lifted it to his lips and placed a soft kiss on my knuckles. His dark eyes never left mine. My eyes widened, and I gulped as the tingle started again, spreading like wildfire up my arm from his touch. Pulling my hand back, I tucked them both in the pockets of my hoodie and looked away from his eyes that seemed to see right into my soul. This apparently made Teagan happy as he gave a little laugh while Hunter scowled back at him.

"I'm sure you're wondering why we're both here. You must have a million questions. As you can see, we're not who you have thought we were, and I'm sorry for that. We were both sent here to watch over you by Celeste. With the upcoming journey, Queen Aine has requested both of us to assist you," Teagan stated.

Of course Celeste sent them too. I wondered if everyone in my life was someone that had been orchestrated by the Moon Goddess. Too bad she wasn't my fairy godmother and could bring back my family. I had so many questions, but before I could ask any of them, Hunter cut me off.

"We're losing time here chatting. We can tell you everything along the way. All you need to know is we are basically your bodyguards. We're here to keep you safe and out of trouble." He looked at Teagan. "Right? Right. Let's go." Impatiently, he gestured to the door, silently shooing me out of the way.

Am I seriously going to have to deal with his attitude this whole time? Oh, this will be SO much fun. I grimaced and backed into the room, allowing them both to step in. That's when I realized what they were wearing.

Teagan wore a black leather suit that reminded me of a ninja. Tight-fitting, with high-tech body armor underneath the suit. He had a ton of weapons strapped to his chest and both legs; they were small but looked deadly. Hunter was wearing something similar, but there were breaks in his suit where velcro held it together. I couldn't imagine why the suit was made that way, but like he said, I would have plenty of time for questions later.

The guys looked around in amazement at the interior of the tree after we filed in. The door clicked closed behind us, and I imagined the looks on their faces were similar to what mine looked like the first time I stepped inside. Balwyn marched up to me with a brown paper package wrapped with twine in his small arms.

"For ya, Miss Andie. Celeste sent these with Eira earlier taday, said you'd be needin' em. They've been magicked to keep you safe from other magic that may be used against ya while in Finias."

He held the package out for me to take. Baffled that there was such a thing as magic clothes, I grasped the package to my chest as I walked over to a small table to unwrap it.

Inside there was a bodysuit, like Teagan's, but instead of black, mine was deep plum. Long pockets lined both legs where I could stash away anything I might need, and the armor inside was lightweight. I wondered what the fabric was made from as I ran my hands over the silky material, and Eira flew around my head.

"Do you want me to put the suit on you, Andie?"

"Um, no offense, Eira, but I can dress myself. I just need a room to change in, please."

She giggled like I had told the funniest joke. "Really, Andie, you've got a lot to learn. Okay, stand still, please."

Before I had a chance to react, she was twirling her finger at the outfit that lay on the table. Sparks of light flew through the air as the suit lifted off the table, and she pointed her finger at me, whispering something before flicking her finger again. A cold, prickly sensation covered my body, and then just as quickly it went away.

"Oh, it fits like a dream! Celeste must have found the best Witchstress around!" Eira breathed as she circled around me, her hands clasped together in front of her, a dreamy look on her face. Looking down, the gorgeous plum bodysuit had replaced my hoodie and jeans.

Wow!

"Dang, Eira! That is so cool! You need to teach me how to do that. Do you realize how much extra sleep I would get in the morning before school if I whipped up some magic like that to put my clothes on? So awesome!" I raved, utterly impressed.

Hunter snorted behind me.

Turning my head to glare at him, he shook his head, smirking. Obviously, he was amused by my excitement. Did I care? Nope! This was just crazy! Teagan sat quietly in a chair watching me, thoughtful as he looked me over. The bodysuit fit perfectly, light and soft, and as I moved to test the flexibility, there was no hindrance to my motions.

"Your suit was designed to repel fire, water, and magic. Any exposed skin isn't safeguarded, though. You need to remember that. Teagan and Hunter will protect what you cannot. Besides being able to fight off anyone attacking you, they will also help you learn how to harness your Fae and Witch powers and teach you how to fight," Eira said as she sat on Teagan's shoulder, playing with a lock of his hair.

Man, these fairies sure liked hair.

"Guys, I'm a little nervous about how I'm going to learn all of this so fast. I mean, I want to learn, but how will I when we've got to start on this mission now?" I asked as I spied Balwyn gathering up packs and placing them on a nearby table. I could only assume they had food and water in them to sustain us on our journey.

Teagan walked over and placed his hand on my shoulder, looking into my eyes. "Most of what you need to learn will come to you once we arrive in Finias. When you cross over, your latent powers will awaken. The knowledge of your Fae powers will be there as if you've always had them in your mind. They were imprinted in you the moment you were born, and only the spell your mom and grandmother cast on you kept them from activating. Your witch powers are a different story. They will activate, but it will take practice to cast spells and learn to fight with your magic. That's where I come in. As a Warlock, I will guide you."

My heart stopped. He was a Warlock. Just like my father. My breath came in fast, and I wasn't getting enough air. This information had caught me off guard and made me excited all at once. I wondered if he knew who my dad was, but Hunter was quick to interrupt as he shoved Teagan's arm off me, inserting himself between us, causing Teagan to move out of the way, frustration wrinkling his brow.

"And *I* will teach you to fight," he rasped, his eyes glowing like they had in the woods. Growling, sharp canine teeth poked out from the sides of his mouth, and long black nails grew from his fingertips. Swallowing hard, I bumped into the table behind me as I tried to back away. His hands balled into fists, and he squeezed his eyes shut, trying to gain control of the transformation. The nails and teeth retracted, shaking his head, his hair softly flew back, before he opened his eyes again, gauging my reaction. I held my breath but slowly let it out in relief.

"Wow... Please don't tell me that's gonna happen to me too," I half-jokingly said to him. He rolled his eyes at me.

"Yes, Andie, you will become a Were shifter..."

At my look of horror, he laughed loudly.

"Don't be stupid. Of course you won't. Only awesome people are shifters." He winked at me as he brushed by, flipping a piece of my hair with his finger.

Inwardly, I sighed. I wasn't feeling the whole changing into a monster thing. I was perfectly fine with being half-Fae, half-Witch.

So many questions for Hunter and Teagan circled around in my head. I wanted to ask about what they are and what they do. Bouncing on my toes to contain them, I watched the guys head over to the table and sling their packs over their shoulders. Eira and Balwyn waited at the foot of the stairs for us to follow. Everyone turned to me with a questioning look.

I grabbed my pack and followed them up four flights of the winding stairs. I tried to be cool, but as we climbed higher, there were more and more things I had never seen before. The second floor was full of books reaching as high as the ceilings on every wall. Tables bore glass bottles with strange embalmed creatures that only existed in nightmares. The third floor was even more bizarre. In the middle of one large wall surrounded by books was a huge aquarium. Something swam around a big rock, and from this distance, it looked like a mermaid! The graceful silhouette came closer to the glass, and long blonde hair billowed out obscuring its face. An iridescent green tail swished back and forth and was mesmerizing. Its hands pressed up against the glass, sharp fingernails scratching against it. As we rounded up to the fourth floor, the creature swiped its hair out of the way, and a long, hideous face, mouth wide open in a silent scream, showing rows of ghastly sharp teeth.

Yelping, I jumped up the final step to the fourth floor, putting the creature out of my line of vision. I couldn't imagine what the other levels of this place hid. Stunned, I knew I may encounter worse things on the journey ahead. At least that one couldn't get to me.

"Don't pay the water wraith any mind, Andie. She's locked in there with magic and won't escape anytime soon." Teagan tried to ease my mind as we followed Balwyn over to a large table in the middle of the room. The fourth floor was thankfully a plain room that looked like a library. All I saw were books and tables.

"G-good to know," I stuttered.

Everyone gathered around a table where a large book with strange leather-like binding rested. Weird letters covered the book. Maybe Greek? It looked to be centuries old, sewn together in patches with strange material. Leaning closer, I realized what the binding was made from, and I gagged.

"Uh... please tell me that isn't made from skin?" I asked with distaste. All of them stared at me like I had asked the most idiotic thing ever. "Oh, come on, I'm new to all of this. Cut me some slack. But skin? Really?"

Eira giggled again, and Hunter tried to hide his grin, while Balwyn and Teagan ignored us. Teagan whispered something in another language, and as his hands hovered over the book, the letters glowed, and the book expanded to five times its size.

"Time ta hold hands, all of ya," Balwyn said calmly, gesturing to the three of us.

Teagan stood confidently between Hunter and me, his shoulder brushing mine, extending his hands for us to take. Looking down, Hunter scowled and slapped his hand away before walking around to stand on the other side of me, just as close as Teagan was. I glanced up at him once he was in place and saw the half-smirk playing on his face. He was so hot and cold, flipping his emotions from one extreme to the next. I frowned at him, but he only smiled wider. He grabbed my hand roughly as Teagan gently took my other.

"Ready?" he asked Hunter and me. We both agreed, and I gulped steeling myself for the unknown. "Remember: don't let go until I tell you," he warned. Closing his eyes and concentrating, he grasped my hand tighter as he shouted at the top of his lungs.

"*Finias oscailte!*"

The pressure built around us and the book was flung open, light pouring out into the room. It felt like gravity had increased tenfold, and as I gripped the guys' hands harder, my vision swam so I squeezed my eyes shut tight. A tugging sensation came next, my body was being pulled forward, and I no longer felt my feet on the floor. Snapping my eyes open wide when a loud clap like thunder boomed all around us, I looked around. The air was thick and musty, and there was nothing but darkness before we were spat out of the portal. Hitting the ground hard, our hands tore apart from the impact, and the breath was knocked from my chest.

Dazed, I heard the guys groaning around me as I lay still trying to get my breath back. Flopping over, my eyes opened to a cloudless purple sky. I thought it was daytime, but the three half-moons in the sky threw me off. I checked to make sure Hunter and Teagan were ok. They both stood watching me, perfectly fine.

My beanie had been torn from my head in the crash, and I was so happy to find it beside me. Worried I might lose it, I tucked it into one of the many pockets lining my suit for safekeeping. I rolled my eyes at both guys as I turned to look around.

We stood in a clearing, much like the clearing where the oak tree stood, except this one was not the same. The grass was brown and dead. The trees surrounding us were bare and looked scorched. Small lizard-like creatures sprinted over the dead branches, and my ears twitched as I realized I heard the skittering of their feet over the bark.

Just then, a sharp pain lanced through my eyes, causing me to cry out. I took my glasses off, pressing my fingers against my eyes, trying to ease the burning pain. I heard Hunter and Teagan arguing behind me, and the pain only intensified.

"*SHUT UP!*" I screamed.

Silence engulfed the forest. The pain eased, and I pulled my hands away, squinting as I opened my eyes. I wish I had kept them shut.

In the dead woods ahead of me, there were weird creatures. All of them standing still, staring. It terrified me. Grouped together, they were bizarre and frightening figures. What stunned me more than the fact they were there was that I wasn't wearing my glasses, and I could see them all crystal clear.

"Guys," I whispered, but they didn't respond. "Guys!" I whispered louder.

Still, there was no response. Afraid, I turned to look behind me. They were still in the same spot from before, but their mouths were sewn shut. Black thread ran through their lips, reminding me of scarecrows I had seen in cornfields. Hunter's eyes showed sheer amusement, but Teagan's were most definitely not amused. He was furious, and it appeared directed at me. He pointed to his mouth and then pointed back to me. Glancing back at the woods, the creatures hadn't moved. Looking back at him again, I pointed at myself.

"Me?"

He nodded and pointed again at his mouth. It took me a minute to figure out that I had done this. When I told them to shut up, somehow, I had literally caused them to "shut up." I looked at them, amazed, wondering how in the world I did that. I knew I had to do something to make them talk again, and the only way I could think of to make that happen was to do the opposite of what I had done before. So, I took a chance.

"Talk!"

Still, they stood there with their mouths sewn shut. Nothing changed. Hunter rolled his eyes at me this time and Teagan shook his head hard, his hair shifting with the movement. He made a gesture with his hand and pointed to me again. So, I guess I was supposed to do that too? It couldn't hurt. I mimicked the motion and yelled again.

"Talk!"

Threads fell from their mouths onto the ground, and they wiped away the rest.

I stared at my hands, amazed. *I* did that? It scared me a little that I was able to do something that might harm someone with a few words. And I would be lying if I said it wasn't a little exciting that I had this kind of power too. It was exhilarating and scary all at once.

"Sorry, guys. I didn't know something like that would happen," I apologized, looking down at my feet. "And, um, I'm not sure if you've noticed, but we've got company," I stated, pointing toward the woods.

"Don't worry about them, Andie. They're not here to harm us. They're more interested in what we're doing here. If they wanted to do us harm, they wouldn't be waiting," Teagan told me. "If you can see them, then your Fae powers have been activated fully. You won't need these anymore either." He plucked the glasses from my hands and put them in one of his pockets.

"Yeah, if they weren't working, you wouldn't see anything strange. It would look like normal woods, normal sky," Hunter added as he gathered the packs that had been thrown away from us when we landed.

Handing them to us, he looked around, his nose twitching as he sniffed the air. "Okay, time to get going. Something is coming, and I don't want to be around when it gets here. We will have to work swiftly to find the Key."

"I wonder what his deal is. I can't ever gauge his mood. One minute he's nice, the next he is aloof or being a jerk," I said plaintively to Teagan as Hunter walked off.

He agreed and looked thoughtful as he and I watched Hunter walk along the border of the woods, taunting the creatures still watching us. They were more restless now with Hunter's actions.

"He's a Were shifter. They're always moody. Don't take it personally. Rarely do they let anyone outside of their pack close to them, emotionally or physically. The fact that he's even here says a lot about his loyalty to Aine and this mission. Believe me, I'm not fond of him either. He doesn't like Warlocks and has taken a real dislike to me."

"Why, Teagan? Why wouldn't all the different groups want to work together? Wouldn't everyone be stronger if they did?" I asked. "I really want to understand how the dynamics of the Fae, Warlocks, and Weres work. You know, newbie here."

Teagan laughed at my response. "Come on. Let's go, or else I think Hunter will freak out on us." He grabbed my hand and pulled me after him. "I'll explain it as we go and hopefully give you enough information to satisfy you."

We followed Hunter to a small path on the other side of the woods, opposite of where our earlier audience had been.

Chapter Nine

We walked forever through the stark, dead woods. Teagan filled me in on all the various groups and how they stayed to themselves, only aiding others when urgently needed. They weren't enemies but never mixed well because of past grievances. Hunter interjected a few times with snarky comments about Warlocks and Witches, but he seemed to have a soft side for the Fae. Which was a good thing, since I was half-Fae.

Rounding the bend, Hunter stopped, throwing his arms out, silently telling us to fall behind. He sniffed the air and growled while Teagan pulled me back further from him. Seeing a large boulder nearby, Teagan put his finger to his lips.

As we crouched behind the large stone, there was rustling in the brush ahead, and I peeked around the rock. A huge black wolf stood in the spot where Hunter had been, his suit in pieces on the ground.

Hunter had shifted to the wolf to protect us.

Covering my mouth, I stifled a gasp at the hideous creature standing in front of him. Boils covered its hairless body, and short tusks curved out alongside a pig-like snout. Its eyes were blood-red, and it had dagger-like talons for fingers. The monster stomped its feet several times at Hunter, and he responded with a roar. Lowering his head and sprinting forward, he jumped at the bizarre thing, raking his claws against its throat, blood spurting out of the deep gash he made. The monster screamed, the noise echoing through the woods, making me cringe as it thrashed without mercy. I couldn't look away from the deadly fight, terrified for what might happen to Hunter.

"We have to do something!" I whispered to Teagan.

Hunter advanced again, slashing his claws at the stomach of the vile creature, before jumping behind it. Confused, the monster stood stunned for a moment before it howled, moving around to face Hunter. It swiped out as he moved backward, and a talon sliced into Hunter's shoulder. The wolf wasn't fazed; he only became more enraged. He engaged the monster in a frenzy, and they battled in earnest, moving so fast my eyes couldn't keep up with what was going on and who was hurt worse.

They rolled around on the ground, arms swinging until Hunter snagged the beast by the throat with his teeth, shaking viciously until it lay limp and unmoving. Rising from the ground, Hunters body twisted and turned, bones and joints cracking as he shifted back into his naked human form. My cheeks heated, and I looked away. Teagan gave me a stern look before walking around the boulder toward Hunter.

"Andie, you can come out now," Hunter called in a jovial voice.

Instant anger bubbled up in my chest at the sound of him so carefree after I had been terrified for him. Charging from around the rock, he had his suit back on, and the strange velcro suddenly made sense. It made it easier for him to shift without destroying his clothing each time.

Deep gashes covered his face and neck, and blood ran in rivulets from them. I worried about the extent of the injuries he sustained that weren't visible to us. My heart stopped at the thought, and in my panic, blood rushed to my head, making me woozy. The guys noticed my distress and were by my side, supporting me before I fell. Both of their faces were grim.

"I'm okay, guys—I swear."

Teagan didn't believe me. The worry in his eyes was heartwarming. Putting his arms under my knees, he lifted me up, carrying me away from the gruesome scene. He carefully sat me down on a patch of dry grass and grabbed a bottled water from one pack, putting it to my lips.

"Here, drink. This will make you feel better," he mumbled, concern etched on his features.

"Really, Teagan, I promise I'm okay. I'm more concerned about Hunter's injuries. Are you okay, Hunter?" I called over my shoulder.

Walking into my line of vision, he stood still for me to look him over. Most of the gashes and cuts on his face and neck were almost healed. Steely eyes bored into mine.

"Please, I'm perfectly fine. Those were just scratches, and they're almost healed. That's the advantage of being a shifter—we heal fast. We don't have to resort to magic to heal ourselves," he said in a cocky voice. "If you think you're well enough to head out, we'd better go. I want to find a secure spot to camp tonight, and I don't need a weakling holding us back." He sneered.

Great. The jerk is back again. Why had I even been concerned about him?

Anger simmered in my chest, and I was about to seriously give him a piece of my mind when Teagan jumped up from beside me, closing the distance between him and Hunter so fast I barely saw him move.

"Man, what *is* your problem? Why do you have to be an idiot and treat everyone like crap?" he asked, getting in Hunter's face. He pointed at Hunter's chest. "Andie has nothing to do with what happened. There's no reason to be a jerk to her. Treat me however you want, I don't care, but leave her out of it!"

I'd never seen him this mad before.

With arms crossed tightly in front of him and an eyebrow raised, Hunter stayed silent the entire time Teagan ranted. But from the look on his face, he'd hit his limit.

"I don't have a problem with Andie. Yet. And you're right, I will treat you however I want. I can't stand you Warlocks, and I won't pretend I'm happy to be here. But I'll do anything Aine asks me to do. To keep our people from perishing, I will do what's necessary," he hissed, turning back toward the path. "Let's go!" he bellowed over his shoulder.

Scrambling, I grabbed my pack and gave Teagan a furtive glance as I followed Hunter. Maybe tonight at camp, Teagan could explain why there was so much bad blood between the two of them.

I tried to keep some distance between Hunter and me as we walked single file down the small path. The further we walked, the more the surrounding scenery changed. Some trees had green leaves, and patches of small white flowers burst through the dead grass. The purple sky was gradually changing to dark blue, and close by, water flowed. Ahead of us, through the dead woods, an abundance of more green vegetation grew. The path ended at a fork, and Hunter stopped, listening and smelling the air. Deciding to go left, he trudged down at a quicker pace. I struggled to keep up; I was worn out and knew I would need to stop for a break soon. My stomach growled, reminding me it had been hours since I last ate. After hiking for a good while, the path ended, and we stood on a stone cliff jutting out over a valley of large red flowers.

Hunter and Teagan looked over the side of the cliff, Teagan's eyes lighting up as he pointed to our right, where a cave opening was nested into the wall. We scrambled over small boulders and brush to get to it. The opening wasn't huge but big enough for us to duck into.

"Stay here, Andie. We'll go inside to make sure it's safe, and that nothing's in there," Teagan said, setting his pack down beside me.

The thought of something lurking in there gave me the heebie jeebies.

"Okay, but if you're not back out soon, I'm coming in to look for you," I stated with a bravado I didn't feel. I already had my fill of excitement for the day.

They ducked into the cave, and I sat on a rock to wait and catch my breath. Looking around, the woods we traveled through weren't visible from this vantage point, only the massive rock face of the cliff that stretched on for miles. High above, there were several other small openings in the rocks. The wind picked up, and wisps of my hair that had escaped the braid flew up into my eyes. As I tucked them behind my ears, a painful pinch on my ankle made me look down.

There, crouched in a defensive posture by my foot, was a fairy. This one was different from the ones in the forest that had been so happy to see me. Armor made of bark covered its body, and its wings resembled dead leaves. The fairy looked up at me with an evil smile and meanness glowed in its eyes. Its grubby little hand held a sharp metal pin.

The pain began to spread through my foot into my lower leg, causing me to gasp aloud as the fairy yelled in a language I couldn't understand, shaking its fist at me. My leg felt like it was boiling from the inside out, the skin around the wound turning a dark red. That stupid evil fairy hopped from foot to foot in glee, watching me writhe.

The pain was so intense I couldn't help but cry out, right as the fairy was lifted into the air, suspended in front of me, its look of glee replaced by horror.

Teagan stood at the entrance of the cave, his hands thrust out in front of him as he chanted a spell. Fury lined his face, determination fierce in his eyes as he glared at the fairy. Smoke curled as flames flickered at its feet before consuming the fairy's entire body. It screamed long and loud before the sound abruptly died. Teagan made a swift motion with his hand, and he flung the dead fairy over the cliff into the red fields below.

The boiling pain spread over most of my leg, making me dizzy from the rawness. Hunter picked me up and ducked into the cave, setting me down gently on the ground to lie with one of the packs under my head.

"It hurts!" I sobbed, holding myself as still as possible because every movement made the fire in my leg ten times more painful. "What's happening to me?" I cried out, fearful as Teagan and Hunter both looked at each other, worry heavy in their eyes.

"It's poison, Andie. That little bugger had a poison dart," Hunter spat angrily.

Teagan reached into his pocket and pulled out a small knife.

"This will hurt, Andie, but we've got to get the poison out. That was a wood sprite, and they kill with poison darts. Hunter, you will have to hold her down." He motioned toward my legs before sitting down by my feet. Pushing my pants leg up, he took the injured ankle in hand.

"Ready?" he asked me, voice filled with confidence. I nodded, biting my lip to keep from screaming in pain. Through the pain, I realized I did something I usually wouldn't do. I trusted him.

"One, two, three!" He slashed a small cut over the wound as Hunter held my shoulders down. I jerked at the pain, and black liquid gushed out from the injury, slimy and foul. That was the last thing I saw before blackness consumed me.

I sat in a chair, my legs tied to it and my arms restrained behind my back. The room was dim, with no light but a few candles, and smelled foul. A woman with midnight black hair stood in front of me, her pointed ears lined with jewels stuck out from between the dark strands of her hair. Her red dress flowed as she paced in front of me. Bare feet peeked out from under the dress as they touched down on the stone floor.

"Now that we have you, I'm not sure what to do with you," she murmured. "You are too powerful to kill, so we must find a way to use you to help us destroy our enemies. You WILL tell us where they are!" She stopped in front of me, bending down to my eye level, her green eyes flashing hatred. Her red lips sneered, and then she laughed, a deep, dark, evil laugh that made my insides quiver.

I would never tell her what she wants. Never!

Disgust for this woman spilled out of my pores, and the energy built inside me, so strong it consumed me. I knew that I needed to let it go before exploding. Though I was restrained, she couldn't keep me prisoner.

My body arched forward, unleashing the power trapped inside of me in a
rush, and the room exploded around me...

There was shouting, but I couldn't tell where it came from. My
body ached, and my stomach rolled. Groaning, I opened my eyes, and
dust motes floated in the air. Small pebbles of rock surrounded me on
the ground.

"She's awake. Andie, can you hear me?" Teagan's voice sounded as
though it came from far away, and I heard Hunter replying to him as
they cautiously approached me. Both had white dust covering them
from head to toe, and a few pebbles fell from their hair as they brushed
themselves off.

"Wha... What happened?" I croaked. My throat was impossibly dry
as if I hadn't had a drink in days. My whole body ached, and my head
was pounding. The dream was still at the forefront of my mind, and
something niggled at my brain that I couldn't quite put my finger on.

"They poisoned you, Andie. Somehow the Fomori found out you
were here and commissioned a wood sprite to kill you," Teagan stated
plainly. He wasn't surprised at all.

"Then how am I still here if they poisoned me? It doesn't seem like
they knew what they were doing at all because it didn't work," I scoffed,
sitting up and dusting the dirt and rocks out of my hair and off my
clothes. Wincing, my body felt like it had been used as a punching bag.

"Are you serious?" Hunter exploded.

He looked at me, and seeing my expression, blew out a loud huff of
air. "You *are* serious. It did work, Andie. You were dying from the poison, and had Teagan not been here to heal you with magic, you would
be dead right now." Turning around, he stormed out of the cave, furious with me.

"Gah, how would I know what happened? I don't know why he's
so mad at me. And anyway, isn't this suit supposed to keep me safe?" I
looked at Teagan, confused.

Squatting down, his eyes were level with mine, his hands clasped in front of him. "That was scary, Andie. You were moments from dying when my magic kicked in, and the spell only worked after Hunter shifted and used his saliva to help heal you faster. We didn't think you would live. The suit keeps you safe, but your ankle was exposed while you sat," he said quietly, looking down at the ground.

I immediately felt bad for acting like it wasn't a big deal. I had no idea what these guys went through watching me almost die and saving my life. I knew I would feel the same way if the shoe had been on the other foot.

"Hey, don't worry, you guys are stuck with me for a long time." I smiled at him as he glanced back up at me.

"I hope so, Andie. We need you... Everyone does." He stood back up as a howl came from outside. I cocked an eyebrow at Teagan, but he shrugged. "He's just letting off some steam, I'm sure he'll be back soon."

While Hunter was gone, Teagan, and I practiced spells. He wanted me to learn as many as possible and explained that while I was passed out, I had gathered all the energy around me, holding on to it until I was so full I couldn't any longer. Not knowing what to do with the energy in my unconscious state, I had released it all at once. The guys had been lucky I hadn't completely destroyed the cave. They had to dig out the cave opening since the explosion had caused the rocks to fall, blocking it off.

I learned how to cast a fire, how to lift a small object and move it, and he taught me how to focus on pushing energy out in various degrees. Teagan was extremely patient with me, answering all my questions, and he didn't make fun of me when I didn't get a spell the first time. I knew that I had a lot more to learn, but at least we were starting to get somewhere.

We practiced for hours when Hunter finally came back. I was reluctant to say I missed him, but I had. He made this mission exciting, and in those rare moments he wasn't growling, he was actually amusing. He was witty and had some excellent sarcastic comebacks. I didn't like to let anyone close to me, but these two were beginning to grow on me.

Hunter strode right up to me with a purpose, looking me dead in the eyes with a fierce expression only he was able to pull off. Frightening and amusing all at the same time.

"Andie, I won't apologize to you for being mad. You have no idea how terrible it was to see you in pain and dying. I wasn't mad at you—I was mad we hadn't prepared you well enough, that we didn't even have the time to do so before throwing you into danger."

His shoulders slumped and his eyes were full of regret as he looked into mine. Patting his arm, I reassured him.

"Hey, it wasn't your fault. I agreed to do this, and you know what? I'll be much more aware from now on after this experience. Teagan has even been teaching me spells, and it's not taking me long at all to get the hang of them. It's almost like I already knew them, like my mind and body were just being reminded of them, you know? It's a little weird, but I guess I'm getting used to it. Now I'm gonna need you to teach me how to fight and defend myself." I smiled shyly at him.

Studying my face, he nodded. "I will soon. Your body needs more time to heal today. It's been through more than it should be able to handle. And to spar with me, you'll need all your strength." He quirked an eyebrow as he looked at me over his shoulder. As usual, his moods were ever-changing.

Teagan magicked a fire in the cave that was smokeless, but the warmth from it was real. We needed it since the cold air from outside blew relentlessly into the cave. My suit kept me relatively warm, though, and I imagined it was because of the magic that was woven into the very fabric. For a while, we sat around like regular teenagers, making jokes and eating some provisions. We tried hard to ration them so we wouldn't run out. We had absolutely no idea how long this journey would be.

Yawning, I stretched out beside the fire, laying my head down on my arm and stared into the flames. I felt so tired, and when I thought about going to sleep, I remembered I didn't have my music to help keep the nightmares away. That reminded me of the dream I had, and I sat up fast, causing the guys to jump up to defend me against some unseen foe.

"Relax," I said calmly, holding my hands up to them. "I just remembered something, and I don't know what it means, but somehow, it has to be significant to all of this." I told them about the woman in the dream, and how I had seen her before at the café. I was cautious not to leave any details out.

Hunter made a disgusted sound and Teagan let out a slow whistle. Both glancing at the other with knowing looks.

"Okay, what is it? I can tell you know something, so spill." I looked from one to the other, waiting.

"It was Freya, Queen of the Elves," Teagan explained, an incredulous look on his face. "We had heard some noise that the Fomori had swayed them to fight against us, but none of us believed she would stoop so low. There's always been a rift between Elves and most of the Fae because Freya has always felt she should have more power in our world. But never in a million years would anyone have thought she would side with them."

"So, this Freya, does she have any sway with other groups? I mean, do you think she would persuade others to join them too?" I asked, thinking ahead to what we might be facing.

Hunter had been silent through our exchange, lost in his own thoughts and probably scheming, but he nodded at my question. "Yes, she does. She was once very close to the Shifters. One of her longtime mates was a Shifter. If she can get to him, he could persuade at least some of them to side with her."

"Is there any way we could persuade her to side with us over them? I mean, there has to be a way to get her to see that joining them would be disastrous," I rationalized. Although, from the way she had acted when we ran into each other, it might be rather tricky. "What would benefit her people the most by joining us? Do you know?"

He shook his head at my question. "Not much. You have to know her, but she's always wanted more power, and she will get that if she joins them. We can't let her have that much power. It would be too dangerous. I'm afraid it will be extremely difficult to get her on our side. We'll just have to make sure no one else joins with them, or they'll be a force to be reckoned with, one I'm not sure we could defeat."

Teagan listened with a thoughtful look. "Hunter, doesn't your father know Freya well? Do you think he could persuade her?" His eyes glinted with something I couldn't figure out as he stared at him. Hunter growled low, a warning to Teagan, who held his hands up. "I'm just saying... whatever will work."

"Listen, you're not helping me any by keeping things from me. If you don't trust me enough to tell me everything and not keep secrets from me, then you both should just leave and let me get on with it," I huffed.

I was worn out, and my body was screaming at me. All I wanted to do was figure out a game plan so we could move forward with this mission. I didn't feel safe being kept in the dark.

"You want to tell her, or do you want me to?" Teagan asked Hunter casually.

He scowled at Teagan but tipped his head in acknowledgment. "I will." Hunter sat with his stare fixed on the ground as he spoke. "Freya killed my mother and then took my father from us." His eyes flashed yellow, anger seeping from him as he spat the words out. My heart plummeted, and I felt genuine sympathy for him.

"I was very young, and my parents loved each other more than anything. They had the perfect relationship. We were happy. Everything in the world seemed right until one day, the Elves visited our pack. They came peacefully, looking for a new place to live, to learn from us, and teach us as well. Everyone got along until Freya showed up. She had a smaller group with her, but all the Elves knew who she was, and they were frightened of her, but wouldn't disobey. She wasn't happy they befriended us and were helping us. Freya tried to take over the first night she was there, but my mother wouldn't have it. She stood up to Freya, and she suffered for it. Freya resented her and would intentionally cause things to happen to my mother. They were jokes at first, causing my mother embarrassment and ridicule. At first, she shrugged it off and ignored it, but the more she did, the more intense Freya's efforts became. One day, when my mother couldn't stand it anymore, she and Freya had an argument, a terrible one." He looked down at his clasped hands.

Taking another deep breath, he let it out slowly. "The next morning, I found my mother by the pond. Her throat was slit, and she was dead." His fists clenched by his side, and his jaw tense with rage.

"No one could prove Freya had killed her. She was very persuasive. She had my father eating out of her hand within days. I tried to appeal to him, to tell him she was behind it all, but he wouldn't listen to me. He was certain someone had stolen into our camp one night and killed her, echoing what Freya was telling all of us. She had him utterly and completely wrapped around her finger."

"That's terrible," I whispered, heartbroken for him. "I can't imagine how you felt to have your father dismiss your concerns. I'm... so sorry." I walked over to him, placing my hand on his shoulder. I knew how terrible it was to lose someone, but to experience what he had was unthinkable.

He looked up at me, his eyes not quite as steely anymore, but pain radiated from them. "It got worse when he professed to be in love with her only three months after mother's death. They were together for years. She was horrible to me, but never in front of my father. Never where others could see and corroborate my claims should I voice them. It wasn't until years later, when she found someone else who was more powerful to latch onto, that she left us alone, and it devastated my father."

My heart ached for him, for what he had been through as a child. No wonder he was so surly most of the time. I swore to myself we would somehow make Freya pay for everything she had done.

For hours, we plotted and planned, but I still had so many questions. I knew we were traveling to Finias to find the Sword of Light; I just didn't know what I would have to do to get it. Hunter and Teagan didn't seem to have any idea either, but both felt sure we'd figure it out on our way.

I was a planner. I liked to know what I was doing ahead of time and what to expect. Not knowing frustrated me.

We finally settled in by the fire, too tired to discuss anymore. It would be a long journey ahead of us, and we needed our strength. As soon as I rested my head on my outstretched arm, I fell into a deep sleep.

"You will conquer those who wish you harm, and after many trials and tribulations, you will save our world. You need to make the correct decisions for this to happen, though. One wrong move, like a house of cards, can make everything come crashing down around you. Use your gifts when possible, but most of all, take the help that is given freely from your allies." The smooth voice floated on the air as I sat in red flowers alone. Dragonflies of all different colors lazily circled above me, and I felt peace.

Chapter Ten

I woke up slowly, but I could have slept forever. The warmth from the fire made me content and warm, and the memory of the dream made me smile. It wasn't often I had a peaceful dream and not a nightmare. Maybe it was a premonition that today would be good.

Throwing my arms into the air, I stretched, my fingers brushing against something above me. Startled, I opened my eyes, and the sight filled me with horror. A hand slapped over my mouth as I opened it to scream.

"Shh. Don't say a word!" Teagan whispered in my ear.

I couldn't take my eyes off the black form hovering a foot above my head. It stared down at me with round yellow eyes and had furry pointed ears that twitched in the light of the fire. It looked like a strange mix of monkey and cat. It didn't seem menacing; it wasn't trying to hurt me. The creature looked at me with intelligence and curiosity in its eyes, gauging my reaction too.

"It's a Phooka," Teagan whispered again, his breath gently blowing on my ear. "He's judging whether you are worth helping. Let's hope he believes you are." His hand slid away from my mouth.

The Phooka floated away from me to settle on the floor of the cave licking the fur on its arms, grooming itself like a cat.

"No, I am nothing like one of those foul creatures." A gravelly voice came from the Phooka as he turned away from his arm, giving me a look of disdain. "I'll thank you to never compare me to one again," he stated, then resumed his licking.

"Uh, okay. I totally agree I was wrong, and you aren't like a cat. Because, um... cats don't talk, for one. They also can't hear my thoughts. That's getting old!" I grumbled to whoever would listen.

"Andie, you'll have to get used to the unexpected. It's all around you now. If everything surprises and irritates you, we will have a long road," Hunter said emphatically from across the cave.

I noticed he had stayed back from the Phooka during the entire encounter, tense and wary, only relaxing once he saw it had made its mind up that I was worthy.

"I know, I know. I'm working on it—I really am." Turning to the Phooka, I had more questions.

"If you don't mind me asking, do you have a name? And are you here to help us?" I asked eagerly, sitting cross-legged on the floor beside him.

He lay down, his head resting on his paws in front of him and his long fluffy tail swishing back and forth. Blinking a few times, he looked at me and yawned.

"Ahh... I have many names, but you may call me Emric. I don't know that I am here to help you, but I am here to make sure you make the right decisions going forward. Is that helping? Some would say so, but alas, some would say no. Only the future knows, only you can tell, and only then will you know if I'm helping," he said in a confusing jumble.

I laughed because as mixed up as his answer seemed, the quirkiness of it delighted me. His mouth lifted on one side as he gazed at me with sleepy eyes in what I could only guess was a Phooka grin. I smiled right back at him, excitement bubbling for what the day would hold.

After packing up and walking outside, I blinked at the brightness from the moons high in the sky. The vivid blue horizon was fascinating to me. Paired with the endless sea of red flowers, the bright colors in this land were incredible. I followed the guys as we walked down a narrow path that would take us to the bottom of the cliff, and into the field of red. Emric followed me, his fluffy tail swishing behind him. After a few treacherous areas where rocks underfoot gave way, and I narrowly missed falling over, we reached the bottom.

The flowers were even more impressive close-up and spanned far. They were taller than all of us, the size of a dinner plate, and their petals looked as soft as silk. I reached up to run my hand over one, and Hunter grabbed my wrist, pulling my arm back down.

"Don't," he said, shaking his head at me as he let me go. "That poison that almost killed you? It's made from these flowers. The petals might not do you any harm, but let's not take a chance, eh?" He winked before turning around.

The wink confused me more than anything so far on this journey. I wasn't sure what to think about the wink, but I acknowledged the butterflies that circled in my stomach. I wished he were nice more often.

Teagan led us through the field of flowers, and again we fell into a single line. I tried to be super careful not to brush up against any of the flowers. I had no intention of going through that pain and agony again. The endless field of flowers made me think of the movie *The Children of the Corn*. Except this wasn't a field of corn, but a field of giant red flowers.

"Hey, Teagan? You've never told me about your family. I mean, I know you're a Warlock, but that's about all." I wanted to learn more, and we all needed something to pass the time.

"Well, my dad is a Warlock and my mother is a Witch. Both are high-ups in the Coven. They're out of town a lot on Coven business, especially now that I'm older. I don't have any brothers or sisters, so eventually, they want to turn over their leadership to me. You grow up fast when from an early age you're expected to lead a large, powerful group. A lot of things are already decided..." He trailed off.

I could only imagine the pressure, knowing he would be the head of some huge magical organization. I didn't understand what all that entailed, but I could see how the responsibility weighed on him already. I wondered what he meant about other things being decided for him.

"Well, hey, at least you know something about your future. Me? I don't even know what I'll be doing, let alone if I'll be alive." For some reason, I felt like opening up a little more to Teagan. Maybe it was because he had been so kind to me, sticking up for me when he felt like I needed him to, or the fact that he had been there for me from day one of this new adventure. But I took a chance, hoping I didn't sound silly.

"You know, I've been thinking a lot lately about my dad. Can you believe he was a Warlock too? I mean, what if you met him one time or another in your Coven? I wonder what he was like, and if he would have liked me had we ever met. Growing up, I really didn't think about him. All I knew was that he left. But now that I know he tried to save my mom and something happened, well, it's opened up a whole lot of questions in my mind."

I glanced at him, and he gave me an encouraging look which gave me the confidence to continue. "What if he's alive? He might be out there somewhere and need help. Or maybe he has been staying away to try and keep me safe. I know it sounds silly, but if he were still alive, I'd want to find him."

Teagan stopped walking, putting his hand on my arm as I stopped too. "Andie, I don't really have any words that could make you feel better. I do want you to know that if there is ever a time you wish to try to find him, I'll help you. I promise." His gray eyes were solemn as they stared into mine.

"Thank you, Teagan. You don't know how much that means to me. One day, I'll take you up on that."

We continued to trudge along. The swish of feathers overhead made me look up at the sky where a raven flew in circles, the black of its feathers glistening in the light. Cawing from high above, the raven appeared to be following our movements. Both Hunter and Teagan glanced up and continued on unconcerned, while Emric emitted a low purr as he stopped to peruse the raven.

"What is it, Emric?" I glanced from him to the bird.

"That, my dear, is a good friend. He is here to be our eyes where we cannot see. You might know him as Charlie." He smirked with a mischievous grin when my eyes went wide.

"But Charlie is a parrot!" I exclaimed, and he bounced his head in a nod.

"Yes, but in this realm, he is a protector and our eyes. You never know when you might need a good pair of eyes, eh? Oh, but some will never say."

I gazed up at the graceful bird, soaring and swooping as if he were dancing in the sky. "Wow. That's amazing. I knew he was brilliant, but this blows my mind." I often glanced up at Charlie as we walked, hoping he continued his peaceful flight, because if he didn't, then something was wrong.

Emric was a funny character. I stifled a giggle after looking behind me several times only to catch him humming to himself and doing a little hop-skip dance as we meandered through the field. Turning back, I ran smack into Hunters back, my arms immediately going to his shoulders to keep from falling. He barely noticed me crash into him but reached back an arm, steadying me. Teagan was in front of him, his hand running up and down through the air.

"What's he doing?" I asked Hunter.

"There's some sort of barrier here. We can't move forward anymore," he murmured

I didn't see any kind of barrier or wall, but looking harder, I saw a slight reflection of ourselves in the air. "It's like a mirror!" I exclaimed. "Can you feel a wall?"

Teagan shook his head, turning to look back at us. "No, but there's an energy there I can feel when I put my hands up to it." He motioned me forward. "Come here and see if you can feel it too. We need to find a weakness in the energy, and once we do, we can spell a doorway."

I moved forward to stand beside him, and he showed me where to place my hands. I concentrated hard, hoping to feel this energy he was talking about. "Yeah, I don't feel a thing, Teagan." I pouted, slinging my hands down to my sides.

"Try again, but this time, quiet your mind. Try to imagine you're in a silent room. Block out any noise. Closing your eyes may help," he encouraged.

So, I tried again. Lifting my hands, I closed my eyes and imagined I was on top of a mountain, and no one else was around. It was beautiful and silent. Slowly, the surrounding sounds dissipated, and a tingle hit my fingertips. It was slight, but it was there. I moved my hands up and down, and the tingle grew. It didn't hurt but was warm, and there was something there.

"I feel it!" I gasped, elated. When I opened my eyes, both the guys were grinning at me, and Emric sat there looking amused, his tail swishing back and forth while Charlie did figure eights in the sky above us.

"Well, well... Let's see what you and Teagan can do together now, shall we?" Hunter gestured at the barrier, impatient as always.

Teagan taught me the words to the spell, which was short, and I picked it up after two or three times. "Now, raise your hands just like before, and put them close to mine. We'll only have a few minutes once we open the door to get through, so everyone will need to hurry."

"You hear that, Emric?" I smirked at him, and I swear he rolled his eyes at me.

"Okay, let's do this!" I said, placing my hands close to Teagan's, and we chanted. The tingle in my fingers grew stronger until it felt like something was pinching them. And then it just stopped, and where our hands had been, a hole in the portal had opened to an entirely different landscape.

We darted through the opening, Charlie the last to swoop through. This place was the opposite of the bright field of flowers. Dark as night, and only one moon illuminated the surrounding landscape. There were mountains in the distance, rising like giants. But around us were rolling hills covered in silver. Reaching down, I expected the silver stuff on the ground to be like glitter but found the texture was cold and damp like snow.

As I dropped it to the ground, snuffling noises came from ahead. Large creatures were roaming the surrounding hills. Straining my eyes, I could see they were like polar bears and just as big. They didn't see us, and if they did, they didn't care. They were more interested in the snow. As they walked around, every so often, they'd stick their noses into the cold silver, root around, and then move on to another spot to do the same thing.

Hunter observed them as only a predator could, and once he decided they weren't a threat, he turned to the rest of us, his hands on his hips and looking every bit the leader. Both guys seemed to take on that role depending on the situation, but I guess that was fitting. Neither one was able to do what the other could, and the strongest one in each position would step up.

"They won't harm us and have no real interest in us being here. Not unless we threaten them. You probably can't tell, but they're foraging for food under the snow." He motioned toward an area close to us. "See that movement over there?"

Gazing at the spot he had indicated, the snow shifted a little before something popped out of the glittery slush.

"That's a lizard. They're everywhere under the snow. That's what the bears are feeding on," Hunter stated.

The one we watched chose that moment to skitter out of its hole and further away from us. Its blue body and white eyes shone in the moonlight.

Ugh. Not a fan of reptiles of any kind.

"Can't we use some spells to magically make ourselves appear on the other side of them?" I joked, but not really. I wasn't looking forward to our trek across the hills covered with these huge white bears and blue lizards.

"Come on, Andie. Just follow us and we'll get through this quick." Teagan smiled at me, holding out his hand. I could always count on him to be calm and collected. Not much seemed to faze him. Hunter, on the other hand, was such a roller coaster of emotions that I never knew where he might land.

Even though I didn't want to, I grasped his hand, gulping as he pulled me behind him and Hunter as we headed off, walking in between the hills, as far away from the grazing bears as we could. Emric pranced behind us, and Charlie soared overhead. He still hadn't called a warning, so I relaxed a little. I kept my eyes peeled to the silver snow, ready to run if one of those lizards popped out at me.

In my head, I sang "Twinkle, Twinkle, Little Star" as we made our way through. The song was fitting because as I glanced up from my feet, stars in the sky came to life, shining bright as they filled the night sky. A few comets streaked by with sparkling green tails. In awe, I stared up at them, my mouth hanging open. They looked so close, almost as if I could reach out and touch them. The stars stretched as far as the eye could see and reminded me of a close-up view of the Milky Way. I never imagined I would view a sight like this, and at that moment, it hit me: I never would have seen these beautiful things had it not been for the circumstances leading up to me being here, and what this journey was about.

"Watch out, Andie. Lizard to your left," Hunter called from behind me, causing me to jump a foot in the air and scramble away. Hunter cracked up, and I stopped running to turn and look at him. He was still laughing, and there weren't any lizards where I had been.

"Ughhh! You jerk!" I yelled, frustrated.

Bending down, I grabbed a fistful of the silver snow and packed it tight, reeling back with my arm and lobbing it at him. It hit him smack in the forehead, exploding in a shower of glitter. He stood stunned, with his mouth hanging open. I laughed with glee, happy I actually nailed my target. What was even funnier was the splash of silver that now covered his forehead and dripped down his face.

Shaking his head, he slung it off, a devious look coming over him. Keeping his eyes on mine, he reached down, grabbing his own handful of snow. I was ready to take off the moment he aimed at me. He reeled back, but instead of throwing it at me, he threw a fast pitch at Teagan, the snowball hitting him square in the chest with a hard thump. I wasn't expecting *that*! Emric sighed and ran off, not at all interested in our childish snowball throwing.

"Oh, you're going to get it now!" Teagan hollered, grabbing two fistfuls of snow and throwing them faster than my eyes could track back at Hunter. One smacked him in the chest, and the other in the shoulder. Before I knew it, we were in an all-out snowball war, running around like loons and laughing our heads off, the lizards forgotten as we played. It was a nice distraction from the mission.

Exhausted, I plopped down in the snow. My suit was waterproof and kept the cold from seeping in, so I didn't have to worry about freezing to death. Teagan and Hunter, both panting, fell into the snow beside me. I saw Emric on a hill, bouncing around. I didn't even want to imagine him catching a lizard and eating it. I had no idea where Charlie had flown off to.

"I don't know about you guys, but I needed that." Teagan breathed hard, before grabbing some water for us all.

"I agree. We did." I sighed, downing my water.

"Where did you learn to throw like that, Andie?" Hunter asked me. "You threw that snowball so fast and accurately. Did you play sports?"

I laughed. Me play sports? Yeah, right! "No, I've never played sports. I'm the nerdy bookworm. I've had no interest in sports."

"I don't think anyone should ever use the term 'nerdy' for you, Andie." Teagan laughed. "You're far from it. Anyway, you don't have to play sports to have good aim. Some people are just naturally good at throwing. And it probably doesn't hurt that your powers helped with that throw too. When you think about doing something, they automatically kick in to help aid you. You won't even be aware of it most of the time."

"Yeah, definitely not nerdy," Hunter said, agreeing for once with Teagan. He started to say something else when he was interrupted by loud squawking in the sky above. *Charlie!* He must have seen something. Jumping up, tense and waiting, we turned our backs to each other, watching every direction. Emric bounded toward us over the hills and slid to a stop beside me on his furry paws.

"Trolls!" He gasped, out of breath from his sprint.

Trolls? Like the toy trolls or the scary under-the-bridge trolls? I laughed a little, and Hunter looked over at me, scowling. "Not the time to be amused, Andie! Get ready. We don't know what they'll do."

A light flickered from behind a hill, and I heard the thumping of feet as they trudged up and over it. How they could make such a loud noise approaching on snow, I had no idea—until I saw the first one as it got closer, flames from their torches illuminating them.

They were nothing at all like I would have imagined. Standing at least nine feet tall, with full, muscular bodies covered in primitive armor. Battleaxes were strapped to their backs, and their skin was dark blue. Some of them had small horns growing out of the middle of their foreheads, while others had longer horns curling around the side of their faces, like a ram. Their skin was pitted, faces full of misshapen features. I counted at least ten of them, more than I thought we could take on, but what choice did we have?

Hunter growled a warning low in his throat, and Teagan held his hands out and at the ready. My heart was beating so loud I couldn't think straight. I wasn't too proud to admit I was frightened of what was about to happen. The trolls marched toward us, and when they were about ten feet away, the one in the lead held his fist in the air, and the group immediately came to a stop. There was a commotion coming from the middle of the group, and the leader turned to see what it was. A soldier held a teenage boy, who was kicking and yelling, by the neck. He was trying his best to break the iron grip of the troll holding him prisoner.

"You're holding someone captive?" Teagan furiously asked. "You must have a death wish."

"Och, what do you know, you wee bugger? We'll kill all ya without no trouble!" the leader bellowed, spittle flying from his mouth and dripping onto the snow below him as he pulled his ax from behind his shoulder.

"Andie, get ready," Teagan whispered from the corner of his mouth. "Remember what I taught you. Think of what you need, and it will happen."

My insides quaked as I realized the battle was about to begin, and I worried about the outcome. Taking a deep breath, I let it out and chanted, pulling energy to me quietly. As I did, I could hear a slow roar start until it became a thunderous noise, and the trolls surged forward. Hunter shifted before my eyes, and in seconds his suit lay tattered on the ground, his huge wolf form flying, ready to tear into them. Teagan's hands lit with a faint glow that grew until a ball of fire was dancing between them. He threw it at the troll advancing toward him. As it made contact, the ball of fire obliterated the giant monster into a pile of ash.

I looked away and realized a troll was stalking closer to me. His evil eyes glowed, and a wicked smile stretched across his face. I frantically tried to think of what to do, but my mind was overcome with fear. As he swung his ax up high in the air, all I could think about was getting out of the way.

The next moment, I was behind him, staring at his back as he looked around, searching for me. I had thought of what I wanted, and it had happened, just like Teagan said! In my peripheral vision, I saw him and Hunter engaged in a fierce battle with at least five monsters. My concentration returned to the one in front of me, who had finally realized where I went. Before he could make a move, I pushed my hands out in front of me, picturing the troll becoming a statue. Energy shot from my hands in white light, pushing into him, and I watched in fascination as gray stone wrapped its way from his legs up to his torso. He fought, trying to move, but the stone kept winding up his body until it slid over his face. The last thing I saw before it completely covered him was his eyes wide with fear.

"Well done, Andie." Emric purred beside me, licking his paw as Charlie cawed, sitting between Emric's ears. I stared at them both, bewildered, before laughing at the absurdity of all of it.

"Thanks, Emric. Can't you do anything to help us?" I motioned toward the large group of trolls wearing Hunter and Teagan down. I could see the strain on both of their faces from where I stood, and I knew it wouldn't be long before they couldn't handle it anymore.

Approaching the group, I picked out the two trolls closest to me and on the outside of the fray. They were the furthest from the guys, and I whispered a spell, blowing it off the tips of my fingers, watching it slither through the air. When it reached them, it formed the smoky silhouette of a giant snake. Both ends of it wrapped around the two trolls' necks over and over again until their bodies fell to the ground, dead.

The leader glanced at them and then stared over at me. Looking around the group, I could see that he realized he had lost more soldiers to the three of us than he had expected.

"*HALT!*" he yelled, his voice booming and echoing off the hills. The fighting stopped as everyone cautiously looked to him. His remaining soldiers awaited orders, and Teagan and Hunter listened, still at the ready to fight should it be a trick.

"Maybe a truce is in order, aye?" he said, scratching his pocked chin with a long nail. "You are stronger than I imagined, and I dinna see how this fight will serve any of us. Shall we bargain?"

"How can we trust you to do what you say? You attacked us for no reason, and you're holding a boy hostage." I pointed at the teenager that was still being held, though he seemed far less combative now. He also appeared to be listening intently to what we had to say.

"Och, tha wee laddie is not a hostage, but a bargaining chip we found along our way to ya." He tapped his head. "We always have a plan fer every outcome, ya see?" He was so sure of himself and that we would follow along with his plans.

"So what bargain do you want then?" I asked, skeptical that anything he came up with would be in our favor.

"Well, I hear ya made an enemy of Freya, but of course ya did. Every powerful creature is an enemy of hers. I'll hand tha young laddie over to ya if, in return, ya promise to come and help us if we should call on ya." His eyes gleamed, and he rubbed his hands together.

"And what kind of help would you want from Andie? Forgive me if I have a hard time believing it would be in her best interest to help you. You're not exactly known for your good deeds," Teagan sneered.

The leader lifted a hairy eyebrow and scanned his remaining soldiers. "'Tis true we find it rather fun to dabble in the mischievous, but we make sure to do a good deed now and then. Right, men?" His fellow soldiers all nodded emphatically at his question, and he turned back to us with his arms outstretched. "See? We mean ya no harm, and if we call on the lass, it will only be with tha best intentions. I, Tinock, promise ya."

Emric wound around my legs, and feathers caressed my hair as Charlie settled onto my shoulder. Hunter had shifted back, and he and Teagan stood close on each side of me. I was surrounded by support.

"Tinock, is it?" Hunter asked.

The leader bowed his head, "Aye."

"Give us a moment to confer, and we'll then tell you what we decide," Hunter stated plainly, watching as the group moved a short distance away. He placed his hand on my shoulder as he looked into my eyes, the worry lingering there. "You don't have to agree to anything, Andie. I'm sure the boy will be fine. They have no need of him and will eventually tire of dragging him along. I don't think agreeing to his request will end in anything good."

Sighing, I looked over at the group of huge warriors. The boy was now on his feet, his eyes pleading in our direction.

"We don't even know who he is, guys. Maybe he could help us with the rest of our mission. If we left him with the trolls, what if they killed him? I can't have that on my conscience. It would eat at my soul, always wondering what became of him."

I rubbed my temples, frustrated. I needed to decide, but I also needed to make sure I made the right one. We couldn't leave this kid here with them.

Rolling my shoulders back, I tried to ease the tension that had bundled there. In doing so, I knocked Charlie off, but he didn't seem disturbed by it. Instead, he fluttered to land beside Emric. His little bird body vibrated before changing into a black panther. Not to be outdone, Emric's body rippled and rolled until an identical panther sat beside Charlie. They smiled at each other, satisfied with their transformations.

I couldn't let the boy stay with the trolls. He needed us, and maybe we needed him.

"I've made up my mind."

I looked at both guys, who had been patiently waiting on me to decide. "I'll agree to his terms and figure out the rest later. Whatever comes, we can deal with it. We just can't leave this kid with them."

Their posture was stiff, and their jaws clenched. Rubbing the back of my neck, I was self-conscious about my choice, but I knew it was the right one.

Finally, Teagan relaxed and smiled at me. "I'm sure this wasn't easy, Andie. And our feelings haven't helped you come to this conclusion. We're just concerned about the outcome and what they may call you to do in the future. I agree, though. We'll figure it out when that time comes."

Emric and Charlie purred before running ahead as I motioned the soldiers back to us.

They trudged over, one of them pushing the boy hard to get him moving. He looked at me with hope in his eyes as he walked closer. His shaggy blonde hair was dirty and hung over blue eyes. His skin and clothes were also filthy, and it looked as if he hadn't had a shower in weeks. He had to be around the same age as the rest of us, but his body looked malnourished and bony.

Tinock stood tall in front of me, his eyes glinting, knowing I would take the deal. He radiated eagerness as I walked over to the boy.

"What's your name?" I asked him.

"Killian," he replied, evading my eyes.

"Killian, I want to help you. Do you understand?" He silently shook his head, quickly looking at me and then away again. "I need to make sure that you understand what I expect of you if I do."

He looked at me again, his face unreadable, and I continued.

"If we help you, I need to be sure you're on our side, that you'll stay with us and help us on this journey. Once we return home, we'll take you wherever you want to go. But this is an important mission, not something to take lightly. okay?"

He agreed, and I swung around to walk back to Tinock. Feigning more bravado than I felt, I stopped directly in front of him, so close I smelled his stench, a rotting, horrible sulfur that made me want to wretch. Somehow, I held it in and stuck my hand out for him to shake. "You've got a deal."

Tinock rocked back on his heels, puffing his chest out and yelled over his shoulder at the soldier holding Killian. "Release the laddie!"

He grabbed my hand roughly, pumping it up and down, and I had to bite my cheek to keep from wincing at the pain it caused. "Dontcha be forgettin' our deal, and I expect you to come whenever we summon you." He sneered before stomping off to gather with his group of nasty soldiers.

Killian walked over to us, looking behind him as if he expected to be grabbed by the trolls again. Emric met him halfway, winding himself around the boy's legs as he stopped to listen to what Emric said. It was probably something nonsensical, meant to impart wisdom. They made their way over to our small group as the trolls took off back over the hills without a backward glance.

Letting go of the breath I had been holding, I realized how exhausted I was. Hunter was beside me in the next instant with a granola bar and some water.

"Here, eat this. Your body is not acclimated yet to using your powers, and you're drained. This will help some. Sit for a minute and rest."

My jaw must have hit the ground at his sweet gesture. This was more like something Teagan would do—not Hunter. I blinked at him, and he grunted, lifting his hand, and with one finger he closed my mouth, his eyes sparkling with laughter.

"Uh-huh... I hate to break up this lovely little scene, but we need to introduce ourselves to Killian. Or he needs to introduce himself to us. Either way, let's introduce!" Emric proclaimed as he flopped down in front of me and laid his head on his paws, giving me a chastising look. Ignoring his attitude, I tore into the granola bar and stuffed it into my mouth before I said something I'd regret. Teagan and Hunter introduced themselves, and they all waited for me as I swallowed the last hunk of the bar and washed it down with water.

"Sorry, Killian. I'm Andie, as I'm sure you gathered before the fight started."

Reaching into a pack, I grabbed another granola bar and water and handed it to him. The kid had to be starving. Who knew if the trolls fed him, and if they had, was it something terrible? I can only imagine the grotesque food they might have, and it made my body shudder. He ate the bar within seconds and was still hungry, but we had to ration as much as possible. Balwyn had only packed enough for three people, so we would no doubt have to forage in the coming days.

"So Killian, how did you get taken by the trolls? We're all curious," Teagan said.

The boy wiped his dirty hair back from his forehead and stared at the ground. He did that quite a lot. Clearing his throat, he looked back up at us, and his blue eyes shimmered with unshed tears.

"The Fomorians raided our village a few days ago and killed everyone except me. I was out in the woods when I heard the screaming. From the edge of the trees, I saw our homes burning, and the Fomorians were killing everyone!" His voice trembled, and he clenched his fist, biting his lip to control his emotions. "I stayed there until they left late that night, and when I went in search of my family, there were bodies and blood everywhere. My parents were dead when I found them."

My heart went out to this kid. The terror he must have experienced at seeing all of this happen and then finding his parents dead had to be traumatic.

"It wasn't long after when the trolls came into our village, pillaging homes that weren't burned down yet, and taking everything, including me."

Teagan leaned down, resting his hand on Killian's shoulder. "I'm sorry that happened. This is proof the Fomori are trying to gain power and take over. We must complete this mission and stop them. Do you think you can help us with this?"

Killian looked at him, his eyes glacial, and his jaw tense. "I will do whatever it takes to end them. Just the way they did my mother and father," he spat, full of hatred.

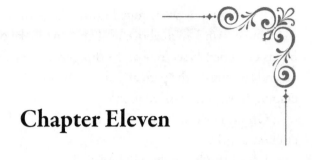

Chapter Eleven

We trekked through the sparkling snow, on high alert for any other sneak attacks. In the distance, I could make out trees. I don't think I'd ever been so happy to see them before. The cold, barren landscape we had spent hours in was wearing on me. Though beautiful, it was empty besides the rolling hills. It was like one of those lovely little snow globes, with only the glittering snow to be seen.

Killian peppered Hunter with questions of all different varieties. There was no rhyme or reason to his questions, but I could tell that he was genuinely curious. Hunter curtly answered the first few, but as there seemed no end in sight to them, he became annoyed and his answers more abrupt. Seeing his frustration and his patience waning, I took up the task of asking Killian questions instead. Hunter gave me an appreciative glance, and I held back my laughter.

As we moved closer to the trees, lush green colors shone in the moonlight. The snow abruptly stopped at the tree line, and a wide path showed the way into a jungle. I was thankful for the width of the trail and not having to walk single-file like we had before. Although Emric and Charlie stayed behind me, protecting my flank while still in their panther forms, Teagan and Killian walked beside me. Hunter took the lead.

Noises were all around us. Birds chirped, bugs skittered, and somewhere, water bubbled. Small and large flowers of every tropical color grew in the trees and all around them on the floor of the jungle. The smell was cloying and robust.

Glancing up as we trudged down the path, I noticed something swinging on vines high above us. I couldn't make out what they were, but as I strained to see, one of the things squealed, flipping through the air and landing on the path ahead of us before running off into the vegetation. It was a fairy-sized monkey!

"Oh my gosh! I want one of them!" I laughed, and Killian looked at me strangely.

"I don't think you do, Miss Andie."

"What? Why not? It was so cute, like a little baby monkey!" I admonished.

Hunter chuckled as he listened to our banter, while Teagan just shook his head at me like I'd gone crazy.

"No, miss, it is NOT cute. Those pests would rip your fingers off one by one, followed by the rest of your appendages, and then feed them to each other. Pintars are not to be messed with. The good thing is that they will leave you alone if you do the same," Killian stated matter-of-factly.

Charlie yawned before adding, "I'd eat them for breakfast before they could even lay one of their puny hands on Andie." Emric nodded his smooth feline head in agreement.

The hilarity of the situation hit me, and laughter bubbled up. I don't know if it was because I was tired, stressed out, had finally cracked under the pressure, or all the above, but I let that laughter roll out of me. It came out in waves, louder and louder until tears ran down my cheeks. I bent over, with my hands on my knees to catch my breath as it finally subsided. Wiping my cheeks, I looked up, my mouth still split in a wide grin. Everyone stared at me like I had lost my mind, and I doubled over in laughter again at their expressions.

"Ohhh, boy. Ha... ha! You guys have got to lighten up!" I exclaimed, getting myself under control again. "Don't look at me like I'm crazy. I just found them funny and had to let off some steam," I said, giggling at the two panthers rolling around on the ground like house cats.

I felt more settled, my heart a little lighter as we began our trek through this tropical place. It fascinated me that there were so many different and dramatic landscapes in this world, each one a stark contrast to the next.

I was lost in thought when Killian broke off from the group, running off the path and into the dense jungle.

"Killian!" Teagan shouted after him as Hunter, Charlie, and Emric sprinted to catch up.

What was going on? Where was he going?

Hunter shifted mid-stride, tearing a path through the thick vegetation. Teagan and I glanced at each other before taking off after them. A path they had trampled through was our only guide.

Breathing heavily, I jumped over a fallen branch and pushed large leaves and flowers out of the way as I ran. Voices came from ahead, and the sound of running water was closer now. When we burst into a clearing, Killian was waist-deep in a clear blue stream with three ladies swimming around him. Their long hair floated in the water as they swirled around, laughing and teasing him. Killian sported a big, goofy grin, and his eyes appeared dazed.

They had to be the most beautiful women I had ever seen. Their faces and bodies were perfect; not one flaw showed. Even more fantastic was how their hair didn't appear wet at all as it floated on the water. One of the ladies moved closer to Killian, running her hand along his arm and laughing.

Hunter growled from the edge of the stream, staring at the women, and Emric tried to get Killian's attention as Teagan and I walked closer.

"Don't touch the water, Andie," he whispered. "The Naiads will lure you in if you do. Killian is under their spell. They must have sensed us nearby and found the weaker one of the group, calling to him.

"We have to help get him out of there! What can we do?" I asked, desperate to save Killian. I didn't save him once, only to leave him here in this stream with these creatures.

"We have to attract his attention, my dear." Emric purred. "The three of them are weaving their magic, and it winds tighter and tighter on Killian the longer he is here. Before long, they'll take him to the bottom of this water, to never come up again."

Killian was just a kid. I wouldn't let anyone come to harm on this journey if I could help it. I wouldn't lose anyone again; I swore to myself. I was determined to find a way to get Killian out of the water and away from these creatures.

"Killian!" I shouted.

All three of the Naiads' heads snapped up in uniform, looking at me with eyes as black as midnight, their facade fading away. Gone were the beautiful, enticing ladies, and in their place floated ghastly wraiths. Bone thin, with skin hanging off their bodies. Soulless black eyes stared from gaunt gray faces. The long beautiful hair was stringy and white, patchy in areas where clumps had fallen out. It was horrifying.

"You do not stand a chance of taking him from us! He is ours now," hissed one of the ghoulish visions. "If you try to take him from us, we will take you too."

Goosebumps ran up and down my arms, and terror at the thought of these nasty things taking me into the depths to kill me made my heart beat faster. I watched as they drew even closer to Killian, crooning something in his ear as they ran their hands over his face and arms. There was no longer a grin on his face. Instead, his mouth was slack, and his stare blank.

No! I won't let this happen!

My spine straightened as anger flared out of every pore in my body. I wanted these sick creatures to die just as horrible a death as they planned for Killian. I imagined the evil in them disintegrating, returning to wherever it had come from, their bodies turning to dust to float away on the current and never harm anyone again.

Energy pulsed through my body. My arms lifted, not of their own accord, and my palms faced the Naiads. My anger was palpable, directing the energy that was burning in me to explode from my fingertips and slam each one of the vile things away from Killian. Their bodies bowed backward until it appeared as if their spines would snap. Their mouths opened wide, wider than anyone's mouth could open. An oily black mist exploded out to curl into the air above them, twisting and turning before disappearing completely. Once the blackness dissipated, their bodies crumbled, white dust sinking into the water.

Killian fell face first once the hold on him was released. Hunter splashed into the water in his wolf form, clamping his teeth gingerly around the belt loop in Killian's pants and pulling him to the safety of the shore. Charlie ran off somewhere. I wasn't even sure when he left, but he wasn't nearby.

Hurrying over to where Hunter had laid Killian on the ground, I kneeled down and took his hand in mine. It was freezing cold, and his skin was blue, but he was breathing. Slow and faint, but it was there, and I was so thankful. Teagan settled on the other side of him as Charlie returned with Hunter's clothes in his mouth.

"We have to keep him warm. Help me with a warming spell, Andie. Just lay your hand on his arm and repeat after me," Teagan advised.

I nodded as Killian's color looked worse.

We chanted the spell over and over, and the warmth radiated from my hand into Killian. After a few minutes of doing this, his color became more regular, and his hand in mine was no longer icy cold. His cheeks now had a rosy glow.

But he didn't open his eyes. "Why isn't he waking up, Teagan? He looks better, but he isn't opening his eyes!" I cried out as emotion welled up within me. Biting my lip to keep from bawling, I shook my head and wiped my eyes. Teagan gave me a sympathetic look; I didn't want his sympathy!

"He will be fine. I promise, Andie. The Naiads drained his energy, so he needs sleep to recover it. We can help him with our spells, but we can't give him strength. That would take too much out of us, and we can't let ourselves fall into any more of a weakened state than we already are."

Hunter came to stand beside us, now shifted back and in his suit. Holding out his hand to me, I silently took it, and he pulled me to my feet. He turned and did the same for Teagan, stunning us both. Teagan stared at the outstretched hand, and I saw the inner turmoil running through his head. Deciding, he grasped it, letting himself be pulled up.

My eyes watered at this profound moment. The emotions from everything that had just happened boiled up again inside me. Hunter slapped him on the back and then turned to me. He looked so much older at that moment.

As if he sensed my need for comfort, he pulled me to him and wrapped me tightly in a comfortable hug, his chin resting on top of my head. I closed my eyes and sniffled, tears running freely. In his arms, I could let them fall with no one else seeing. After a few minutes of blubbering, I was all cried out. Hunter pulled back, holding me at arm's length, and reached out to wipe stray drops that lingered on my cheeks.

"Feel better?" he asked in a gravelly voice, concern shadowing his eyes.

"Yes, I actually do. Thank you. I'm sorry about that. I'm not usually very emotional," I said. I could hear snickering in the background, and looking over my shoulder, Emric and Charlie stopped when they saw my glare. I could tell they were holding in their laughter. I shook my head and looked back at Hunter gratefully before pulling away.

"Hush, you two," I stated, biting my lip to keep from laughing at how silly they looked rolling around on the ground with goofy looks on their fierce feline faces. Sitting down next to Killian, I pulled my knees up to my chest as Hunter and Teagan also took a seat nearby, all of us taking a break while Killian rested.

"So what else can you two change into?" I asked Emric and Charlie. "So far, I've seen Charlie as a parrot, a raven, and now a panther. Emric, you've been a Phooka and a panther. Can you change into whatever you want?"

Charlie rolled over onto his stomach, stretching, his sleek fur ruffled. "Yes, we shift into whatever form suits our situation. We've been many things in our lifetimes and can adapt very quickly." His voice was raspy and rough, but it didn't bother me.

"That's pretty cool. Too bad I can't do the same. I imagine it comes in handy in situations like this."

After he had been silent for a while, I noticed Teagan was staring at Hunter with a look I didn't understand. His eyes shifted back to me, his brows lowered, and eyes intense. "You'll be able to change into other forms eventually, Andie. Once you harness your Witch powers, you'll be able to shift. Maybe not into as many forms as Charlie and Emric, but you *will* be able to change."

This information perked me up, and I started daydreaming about all the different things I wanted to shift to. I know I had teased Hunter before, but the more I thought about it, the cooler it sounded. Could I be a dragon, breathing fire at my enemies? Or maybe a cheetah that could run faster than lightning? Either way, the fact that I would be able to eventually shift, lifted my spirits and excited me.

Killian seemed to breathe easier now, and I had no idea how long he might sleep. Our group was silent, each of us lost in our own thoughts. The sounds of the jungle surrounded us, but I felt relatively safe for now. The recent events had caught up to me, and I stifled a yawn, blinking my eyes several times to keep them open. Emric and Charlie snuggled together, having fallen asleep some time ago.

"Rest, Andie," Hunter whispered as he leaned over to put his pack on the ground. "I'll keep watch for now." He looked at Teagan, who was resting against a tree, his eyes closed.

"Are you sure, Hunter? I can stay up and help you." I yawned again, covering my mouth with my hand.

He laughed and shook his head at me. "Go ahead. I'll be fine. I'll wake you after Killian wakes up. And Andie? You did fantastic back there." Gesturing to the pack, and for me to lay down, his eyes shone.

A little nap wouldn't hurt, and I knew there was no way I could help defend our group if I didn't rest. Resolutely, I laid my head on the pack, curling into a ball, and soon fell asleep.

I slept fitfully, tossing and turning, dreaming that something was chasing me through the green jungle, but I couldn't make out what it was. Just when it seemed as if it might catch me, I heard it calling my name.

"Andie! Andie, shh. It's okay! Wake up." I woke with a start, sitting up quickly, only to smack my forehead against something hard. "Ow!" I rubbed my hand against the spot on my head that had hit what felt like a brick wall and peered out from under my hand to find the offending object.

Hunter rubbed his cheek gingerly. Thankfully, he didn't look mad about it. His eyes danced, and that half-grin finally made an appearance again as he chuckled. "You sure do pack a punch, Andie."

"How was I to know your cheek was in the way?" I scowled, making him chuckle again. His eyes darted to the side. "We have a guest. I thought it best to wake you up. You were tossing around something terrible in your sleep."

Teagan, Emric, and Charlie were speaking with an older man, and Killian watched from where he sat on the ground, awake now. The man didn't look to be Fae. He looked human to me. But really, how was I to know anymore?

His salt and pepper hair was shoulder-length, and a short beard graced his strong jawline. As I studied him, he looked straight at me with piercing sapphire eyes that reminded me so much of Celeste's. His clothing was pretty normal. Jeans, a button-down black shirt, and loafers. Who the heck was this guy?

Keeping his eyes on mine, he stood, pushing through the group, intent on making his way over to me. He stealthily approached, his eyes never leaving mine. I looked down at those shiny loafers as they came to rest in front of me, and he squatted until we were at eye level.

"Hello, Andie." He dipped his head as I stared up into his face, confused. "My name is Coeus. Aine informed me of your quest, and I had to come and see you for myself. Never in my wildest dreams would I have expected someone like you."

His statement made me bristle. "Do you mean it surprises you that a girl is taking this on?" I asked, biting the inside of my cheek to keep from spitting the words at him. "I'm not sure what you're getting at, but please do tell. We haven't got a lot of time to waste." I stood up, not willing to be inferior to him.

He stood also, his height still looming over me, but at least I didn't feel like a child being talked down to. His face lit up, and a brilliant smile showed through his beard. That look again reminded me of Celeste. She always had the same look after reading my thoughts. I groaned out loud, which only made him laugh again.

"You, my dear, are something special. I must apologize. I meant nothing rude, but I can understand how you misconstrued it," he said sincerely. "I only meant to say that I had never expected someone so full of light, hope, and talent. Your combined powers may not be yet at their full potential, but they will be very soon, and you will be extraordinary." He reached out and cupped my face in his hands, then spoke in a resonating voice, the flecks of blue in his eyes swirling as I gazed into them.

"You are nearly to the first Key, and treachery is around every corner. Do not doubt the strength that you possess in your mind and your heart. It will not let you down. Be confident in your choices, for only you can make the correct ones. And always, always remember you are not alone in this fight."

As he spoke, the present had fallen away, and I saw snippets of events in my mind, like photographs snapped in quick succession. Some terrified me, and the others elated me. I was not sure what to make of them all. However, a sense of calm came over me as each one passed in my vision.

When they had played out, I returned to the here, and now, Coeus still stood in front of me, his hands clasped casually.

Clearing my throat, I asked the burning question. "What are you, Coeus?"

Behind me, I could hear Teagan coughing, and I turned to see what his problem was. He was fine after having choked on the water that he was drinking. Raising my eyebrow at him, I turned back, waiting for Coeus's answer.

He seemed amused when he finally spoke. "You would not have a reason until now to know who I am, and it's really of no consequence. Just know that I came here to give you the visions that you just received. They may come in handy in the future. And this."

He reached into the pocket of his shirt, pulling out a silver bracelet. Extending it toward me, he indicated that I hold out my arm, and I let him slip it on my wrist. The silver metal was cold against my skin, and there was a small, intricate metal dragonfly in the center of the bracelet. A diamond graced each wing, glinting in the moonlight.

"It's beautiful, but I don't understand what it's for?" I questioned.

"Darling girl, this bracelet is charmed by the gods. Dragonflies strip away the negativity that holds us back, and they are the keeper of our dreams. They help us navigate transformation with power and poise. But most of all, they represent our journey from darkness to light. This symbol will help you when it is time for you to transform, and it will also keep the darkness at bay. As you get closer to each Key, it will light up to let you know you are on the correct path. Never take it off. Do you understand?"

I admired the beautiful jewelry on my wrist, and then I realized that the bracelet had tightened around it. Not uncomfortably so, but it definitely had formed to my skin, the diamonds slightly glowing. My eyes were wide as I looked back up at him.

"I understand. Thank you," I whispered in response, not knowing what else to say, and feeling embarrassed, I bowed my head and stared at his shiny shoes again. I could feel his hand on the top of my head as he whispered words in a different language. When he was done, he lifted my chin, bringing my eyes to his. "If you come upon a circular doorway made of branches, make sure you go through it. Tell it where you want to go, and it will take you there. It is imperative for your journey," he stated with no-nonsense before grunting and turning to walk away.

"I'll check back on you and your team, Andie. You may not see me, but I will be there," he called over his shoulder as he faded into the lush plants that grew around us.

Chapter Twelve

I looked around at all the guys as they stared after Coeus. "Okay, someone want to enlighten me? Who or what is Coeus? His answer wasn't exactly forthcoming."

They chuckled as they turned back around from watching him leave, and Killian raised a sardonic eyebrow at me. Was I the only one who didn't know who he was? I was frustrated, and I didn't enjoy being left out.

They seemed to enjoy my reaction and were stretching out the suspense until I couldn't take it anymore. I stomped my foot on the ground like a toddler, my fists clenched by my side, and I frowned at them all. "Come on, guys!" I whined. "Stop with the suspense and tell me who he is!"

Killian took pity on me, coughing before letting the cat out of the bag. "Andie, Coeus is the wisest of the Titan gods, a god of Intellect and Prophecy. You received a rare and great honor being visited by him, and given a gift no less." He grinned like a little kid, wonder still fresh in his eyes.

"Wait a minute... A god just came to me and gave me advice and a gift?" I looked at each of them, and all they did was stare at me, mirth dancing in their eyes. I knew they were enjoying this.

"One of you could have told me! I probably made the biggest idiot out of myself in front of a Titan god!" I groaned, covering my face with my hands, embarrassed and mad at the same time.

"Nah, you didn't make an idiot of yourself in front of him, Andie," Killian offered. "If you did, he sure wouldn't have given you that bracelet." I looked at him gratefully, glad for the boost of confidence. The other guys nodded in agreement, and it somewhat made me feel better.

In all the excitement of Coeus's arrival, I'd forgotten about Killian and what he had been through. Abashed, I rushed over to him to kneel and run my hand up his arm in concern.

"How are you? Do you feel okay?" I looked over my shoulder and called Teagan and Hunter, asking them to grab some water and a granola bar. Nan had always fed me when I was out of sorts, and I wanted to do the same for Killian. My stomach twisted with worry for him.

"Relax, Andie. I'm great. I promise!" He gave me a chastising look, but I didn't care. After spending time with him, we had a connection. If I had a brother, I imagined he'd be like Killian, and I had a strong urge to protect him. When I was satisfied that he was fine, I sat back on my heels and smiled.

"Okay, okay. But you're going to stick closer to us from now on. Nothing like that can happen again, got it?" I said as sternly as I could before standing back up and ruffling his hair.

I felt renewed, with a new sense of purpose. Staring down at the dragonfly bracelet on my wrist, I realized that I couldn't do what I needed without the rest of this group. I needed them to teach me everything to be able to find and procure the first Key.

With a new resolve, I moved to where Hunter was standing, his pack slung over his shoulder, ready to get back on the move. I stopped right in front of him, looking into his eyes, so he could see how serious I was. They smoldered into mine, and my heart beat a little faster. Our friendship had become more complicated, and I finally acknowledged that I had a slight crush on him. He had that mysterious bad boy aura that drew me in. But I think the kindness that he tried so hard to hide was really starting to get to me.

I swallowed hard and pushed those thoughts to the back burner. I didn't have time now. Maybe never.

"I need you to teach me how to fight. Now. I can tell you're ready to go, but I feel helpless, and I need to be sure that I can contribute other than magically in a fight if I must. Your lives and mine might depend on it sometime, and I want to be ready," I said firmly.

He was quiet as he studied my eyes, just like I had expected he would. Once he was satisfied with what he saw, he nodded stiffly, all business now. Laying down his pack beside a large rock, he sauntered behind me. His eyes never left mine, like a lion stalking his prey. I stood stock-still and waited to see what he did.

In the next instant, I was grabbed around the neck roughly and pulled back hard into his muscular chest. I started struggling, pummeling his thighs with my fists and kicking my feet back at his legs. He didn't budge, continuing to apply pressure to my throat with his forearm, and I had a hard time even gasping for breath. Throwing an elbow back, I connected hard with one of his ribs, and he growled low into my ear, increasing the pressure.

"That was a good hit. Next time, use even more force and stomp on my foot at the same time," he told me, releasing the tight hold around my neck, and I bent over coughing, my face flaming. He hadn't been easy on me. Part of me was mad, and the other part of me rose to the challenge, ready to go again. Glancing over at the others, I noticed Teagan was grim, his arms crossed tightly in front of him, and Killian's eyes were as round as saucers.

"Okay. Show me more," I hissed, pumping myself up for whatever fresh pain awaited me.

With a gleam in his eye, he laughed. "Try not to be so much of a girl this time."

Narrowing my eyes at him, I huffed in anger. *Oh, it's on now!*

"Try to take me down, Andie. Knock me to the ground." He jumped around like a boxer before a fight, motioning me toward him.

Taking a big breath, I rushed at him, intent on jumping on him as hard as I could and hoping the force took him down with me. At the very last possible moment, he moved faster than my eyes could process, and I flew forward into large green leaves and hit the ground hard. Pollen from the surrounding flowers floated over me in the air. As the sticky yellow fluff landed all over me, Emric and Charlie pounced into the flowers, sending another round of pollen flying. Their fur instantly coated with yellow. Rolling around like two toddlers would in a pile of leaves, they were having the time of their lives while I was still trying to gather my wits back to me.

I looked over at the playful cats and saw Hunter leaning against a tree, picking imaginary dirt out from under his fingernails. One of his eyebrows shot up as he looked over at me.

Frustrated with myself and him, I decided to give him a taste of his own medicine. I was so tired of his cocky attitude, especially now, when I was actually trying to learn. I searched my mind for words that would rhyme to make a spell. I had no idea what I was doing, but it couldn't hurt to try. Right? The perfect words popped into my mind. I hope I don't screw this up.

I slyly grinned at him as I mumbled the words low. I didn't want him to hear the spell and try to stop me. As my lips moved, his self-assured demeanor changed to one of confusion.

Big Bad Wolf, with sharp fangs, let him change with a bang.
Make this big black kitty walk around singing a ditty.

Pushing my hands out into the air in front of me, a tingle of power shot out of my fingertips heading straight for Hunter. Emric and Charlie stopped their roughhousing and went still as they sensed the magic. A little too late, Teagan shook his head with a frantic look as the spell hit Hunter, causing him to flinch.

The strain showed in his eyes as he clamped his mouth closed, fighting the spell. The rest of us were silent, and the whole jungle was holding its breath. Birds stopped their songs, and the bugs went quiet.

I watched as the corners of his mouth twitched, and one side of his lip curled up as he fought to keep his mouth closed.

His eyes screamed murder at me, and his fists clenched. Losing the battle, his mouth opened, and he belted out a song. Never had I heard a worse attempt at "Simple Man" by Shinedown. I gritted my teeth at Hunter's off-key rendition, thinking maybe I should have picked a different spell.

His eyebrows lowered over eyes that radiated anger. As he continued to sing, he pointed his finger at me, shaking his head. Killian stood by the edge of the clearing, out of Hunter's vision, with his arms wrapped around his waist and a huge smile stretched across his face. Teagan's was pale, and he stood as if ready to intercede.

I was still shocked that my spell worked, and the hilarity of the situation, despite the awful singing, hit me, and I burst out laughing. Dusting off the sweet-smelling pollen as I stood up, still chuckling, I peered out from under my lashes at Hunter.

Laughing had obviously not been a smart idea.

Hunter stalked toward me as he continued to sing. Realizing that he was seriously mad and coming after me, I squealed and ran as fast as I could to the other side of the clearing where Teagan and Killian watched.

"Teagan! How do I stop the spell?" I panted, my adrenaline high.

Hunter's eyes turned to the wolf's yellow as he reversed course, now stalking toward the three of us.

"Andie, I tried to stop you! Hunter hates to sing and hates music. You've done it now."

Hunter was almost upon us. Sauntering in front of him, Emric brushed his tail against Hunter's leg, muttering, "Spell, spell, spell be gone! Back to which ye belong."

I swear Emric rolled his eyes as he looked up at me. *Ugh. Now even this joker thinks I'm stupid.*

Hunter immediately stopped singing, leaning over to spit into the grass beside him as if the spell left a disgusting aftertaste. He glared daggers back at me with fire in his eyes, and my stomach clenched at what I had done.

"Hunter, it was a joke. I swear! I got tired of all your sarcastic comments and just wanted to give you a taste of your own medicine. I didn't realize it would make you this angry. I promise!"

Holding my hands out, I pleaded with him to understand.

Grabbing my hands in his much larger ones, he yanked me right up against his body, his breath warm on my face as he huffed. Anger radiated off him.

"Never. Ever. Mess with my free will again! This time, I'll overlook your ignorance, but a second time and you won't be happy with the consequences."

As he said the last sentence, he leaned in closer, as if getting in my face would help make his point. Inadvertently, his lips grazed mine, causing us both to jump back as electricity bounced between us. His steely eyes pierced mine while his heaving breaths slowed, and the tension he held onto dissipated.

My heart stuttered as he turned and stalked off.

"Awkward!!" Charlie squawked as he flew by me, back in his parrot form. His words echoed my feelings. My face flamed. I was so embarrassed and furious all at the same time. How could I have known the spell would cause all of this? How was I to know that he wasn't a good sport? I was so conflicted, so many emotions flowing to the surface.

"Andie, I'll go talk to him," Teagan said, putting his hand on my arm and turning me around to look at him. "He'll be fine. I promise."

There was second-hand embarrassment for me in Teagan's eyes, and Killian sat with Emric and Charlie, trying to appear as if he wasn't paying us any attention.

"Dang it, Teagan! Don't try to make this better for me! I did this. I was so stupid. Just when I thought I was making headway with him,

I do this and screw it all up!" I vibrated with anger at myself, and all I could think about was getting away to be alone.

I did just that.

Stalking off into the jungle on the opposite side that Hunter had, Teagan yelled at me to wait. But I wasn't waiting. I needed time to think, and I couldn't while surrounded by all of them.

I wandered aimlessly for a while, not really paying attention to my surroundings or where I was going. I was so lost in my own thoughts and replaying what had happened in my head that at first, I didn't notice what crept up behind me.

Looking over my shoulder, a pure white fox with bright blue eyes flashing watched me. Its eyes reminded me of something, but I couldn't quite think of what it was. Determining that the animal was just traveling through the forest, I continued walking, keeping it in my vision.

"So what are you doing out here, foxy? Did you tick someone off too? Misery loves company," I prattled aloud. Who knew? Maybe it was like Emric and could understand me. After a while of mindless chatter to the fox, the snow-white animal grew bored, cutting away from my path, running into the surrounding vines.

"Well, bye to you too!" I shouted, stopping to lean down with my hands on my knees to rest. I had been walking forever.

Checking out my surroundings, shock rolled through me. Strange objects hung in the trees around me. They looked to be made of a strange gossamer material, twine running around the bases, holding them onto the tree limbs. There were holes in the front that could only be doorways, and small bridges made from twigs and twine spanned the distance between each dwelling. All around me, I heard the soft hum of wings. Looking higher, fairies darted in and out of a large Alder tree carrying tiny wooden buckets. As one fairy flew overhead, a small drop of something splashed out of the bucket it carried, landing in front of me on a leaf, staining it red as it slid down.

I leaned down and ran my finger over the red substance, studying it. The fairies must harvest the red sap from the Alder tree. I wondered if they were using it as a dye, or for something else?

Watching the fairies work, I noticed that they resembled Aines fairies, but these were not as elegant as hers. They reminded me of worker bees, zipping in and out, working ceaselessly with their buckets, and I swear I heard one of them shouting orders to the others.

Right then, the white fox appeared on the other side of the Alder tree, peeking out at me with a look of amusement and satisfaction in its intelligent eyes. Moving closer to the tree, I trampled a bunch of small branches that littered the jungle floor, keeping my eye on the fox as I walked. There was a cracking noise, and then I was falling before being plunged into darkness.

Shock coursed through my body as I splashed into cold water. My body rocketed down with the momentum, and I had an errant thought about how lucky I was that I hadn't taken a mouth or nose full of water when I hit. My descent through the water slowed while my lungs burned, aching for air.

Kicking hard with my feet, I pushed my way up, or well, I hoped I was going up, anyway. It was forever before I finally burst through the surface, gulping air greedily. Something scaly brushed against my calf and I panicked, turning circles in the water, searching for what it was. I couldn't see anything but bright blue water glistening, and I realized that I was in an underground cave. Vegetation grew around the side of the pool, thick like a jungle. How was that possible when the only light I saw was what filtered from the hole that I fell through?

Staring up at it, the white fox peered down at me, and a woman's gentle laugh rippled through the air before it turned and ran off. It was then that I knew the fox had been leading me here for a purpose, and it couldn't be a good one.

Knowing that something was in the water with me, I swam over to the shoreline as fast as I could. Pulling myself out onto dry land, I was happy that the air was warm and humid. My body was cold all the way down to my bones. After wringing the moisture from my hair and clothes as best I could, I decided to see if I could find a way out of this strange place.

Large mushrooms of every color grew amidst the tropical plants, some spongy growths glowed like lanterns. It felt like I was in some alternate *Alice in Wonderland* story, where I didn't fall down the rabbit hole, but a fairy hole. As I gazed around, there was a faint splash, and glancing back at the water I saw a creature resembling a horse. Its backside had a tail covered in multi-colored scales, and its mane was a spiked fin.

A Kelpie!

Stunned, I stared as it languidly moved in circles through the water before plunging deep and disappearing. Tales about Kelpies always said that they drowned mortals, and I felt fortunate if that was true.

All righty then.

Sighing, I turned back around to start my exploration and hoped that I would find a magical doorway that would lead me out of this quiet, fantastical cave. As I walked deeper into the jungle, there were more of the cocoon homes suspended throughout the trees. They seemed to be unoccupied for now.

A huge white flower caught my attention below the base of the trees, and the smell from it drew me in. The velvet white flower was the size of a platter, and its aroma reminded me of cotton candy. As I stood before it, leaning down, I breathed in the heady fragrance. Within a second, the flower moved, its stamen shooting bright pink pollen into my face and up my nose.

Stumbling back, I wiped at my nose with both hands.

What the heck?

I tried to clean the sticky substance off my face when I became woozy, my vision blurry and my legs swaying beneath me. That was when the buzzing behind me grew, and I fell.

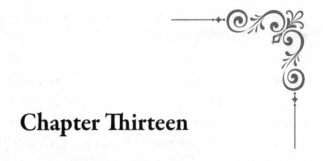

Chapter Thirteen

A tinkling of voices awakened me, and shifting, I rolled onto my side. Whatever I lay upon was soft and squishy. My head pounded and my eyes were sticky and out of focus. The buzzing of voices around me became clearer as my hearing and vision sharpened to normal. I was surrounded by fairies, their wings fluttering as they hovered around, all eyes focused on me.

They had dirty faces and clothes made from brown leaves smudged with dirt and sticky red sap. They went silent once they realized that I was awake. I studied them as they peered down at me, realizing that they were no longer tiny. How had they grown to be the same size as me? How was that possible?

Sitting up, I immediately realized that had been a bad idea as my stomach rolled, and its meager contents rushed up.

Groaning, I leaned over, vomiting. Hands held my hair back gently, and I could sense a soft breeze on my hot neck. Once my stomach stopped cramping, and I felt as if I had purged a week's worth of food, I opened my eyes, and instant vertigo hit me as I looked down from the platform to see the jungle at least fifty feet below me. How did this happen? The inside of the cave hadn't been that tall before.

"Don't move too fast. The pollen from the candlewig flower is strong and may take time to purge from your system."

To my left, a slight fairy hovered, her dirty hands clasped together in front of her. Brown hair stuck out in haphazard disarray from under a cap fashioned from a leaf. The end curled up above her right eyebrow, giving it a jaunty look. Bright green eyes stood out amongst all the brown, and her stare was concerned.

My mouth worked to form words, but nothing came out. The green-eyed fairy girl was elbowed aside by a short male fairy who sneered down at me. His dull brown eyes flashed hatred, and his lips curled up in an ugly smile.

"Don't coddle this one, Lunafae! You can't keep her. You know the plan! We will never be free if we don't follow through with this, so keep your bleeding heart out of it!" He ground out as he looked at the kind girl.

Lunafae scowled at him, her eyes flashing fire, contempt for the sleazy male fairy oozing from her pores. He didn't seem to notice or didn't care if he did. Pushing her way back over to me, she swept one hand out to keep him from getting closer while reaching down with the other to help me up.

I gained my footing only to sway on the smooshy landing. It looked like a giant mushroom, red with white spots. Lunafae grasped my shoulders to steady me, and leaning forward, she whispered in my ear.

"Do not worry. I will get you out of here, but for now, you have to go along with this."

I schooled my features so as not to give her away. The ugly little mean fairy stared at the two of us, his hands on his hips while his wings fluttered erratically behind him.

"Right. Well, let's take her to a room and get her ready then!" He clapped his meaty little hands and then flew up into the air toward a group of trees with lights twinkling through them.

Grabbing me around the waist, Lunafae propelled us both into the air. As we soared, fright at my predicament was replaced temporarily with exhilaration at the sensation of flying. Even if I didn't have wings, it was a magical feeling that I sure could get used to!

As we got closer to the large copse of dark trees, I saw more of the hive-like homes hanging all throughout. Lantern light illuminated them in the dark and created a cozy scene. The last few minutes had been a whirlwind, and my mind hadn't caught up with the fact that the fairies and I were now the same size. Everything in this cave seemed to be twenty times the size it had been before. Something weird had happened.

Clearing my throat, I whispered over my shoulder to the fairy. "What happened to me?" I glanced around at the other fairies who flew around us, making sure they hadn't overheard. I didn't want to get Lunafae in trouble.

"It was a candlewig flower. Its pollen changes your body make-up to that the size of one of us," she stated quietly. Her words caused a shock to pour through my body like ice, making it first hot and then burning with the knowledge. A million questions flew through my mind, but we were swiftly approaching a home. I would have to wait for a better opportunity.

The soft landing surprised me. I wasn't jostled at all as I had expected. Lunafae led me inside, pushing the fabric hung in the doorway aside as we entered a room at the back of the home. I wasn't afforded a chance to look around.

An older fairy stood beside a table waiting patiently. She was significantly cleaner than the others I had seen in the cave. Her leaf dress was long, and her short hair was a fiery red, her eyes a sparkling emerald just like Lunafaes. I decided she must be her mother; they looked so similar.

Both women sat me down and explained they needed to prepare me for a meeting. Their eyes pleaded with me to not ask questions, and I knew they were trying to keep others from hearing our conversation. The walls on these homes seemed fragile, not constructed with privacy in mind.

A large tub steamed with water, and they directed me to undress and get in. I was hesitant because I really wasn't fond of taking a bath in front of anyone. Sensing my embarrassment, the older woman spoke up.

"Dear, you have nothing to be embarrassed about, but if it makes you feel better, Luna and I will leave the room and give you some space to wash up."

Luna, huh? That seemed infinitely easier to say than Lunafae.

"Thank you, ma'am. Um, what's your name if you don't mind me asking?"

"I am Sola, and this is my daughter Luna. We need to hurry before Jasper returns," she whispered to me.

"Okay, I promise I'll hurry. But I am curious why that mean little fairy was calling your daughter 'Lunafae.'" Sola had a look of distaste on her face when I mentioned what the little jerk had called Luna, and I could tell there was no love lost at the thought of him.

"Jasper calls her that because she isn't like him, and he detests it. She and I are not the same as Jasper, but that is a discussion for another time. Come. Get in the bath, and then we'll get you dressed when you have finished."

She and Luna walked through the fabric covering the door, leaving me to clean up and get ready for whatever was to happen. After taking off my suit, I placed it on a small table by the side of the tub. I tried to take off my bracelet, but it wouldn't budge. As if it had fused directly to my skin. Shrugging, I dipped my foot into the water, and bliss ran through me at the feel of the warmth. I hadn't been able to wash since we began this journey, and it felt so good. Sliding down into water up to my chin, I closed my eyes for a moment, breathing deep to calm my thoughts.

I wondered if the guys were out searching for me and if they worried about me. I knew Hunter had been mad, but I could only hope they would find me soon. We still had a job to accomplish, and I couldn't make sure that happened if I didn't get out of here.

Reaching for a bar of soap that sat on the side of the tub, I washed my hair. The soap smelled like apples and was pleasant. Although I'd never used bar soap on my hair before, it looked to be all they had.

Once I was done, I quickly got out and found a fluffy towel hung over the back of a chair. It wasn't really a towel, but made of some odd green material woven together. It smelled like the woods, fresh and clean, and soaked up the moisture better than any towel I'd ever used. Studying it as I dried my hair, I realized it resembled moss.

It was strange, but hey, whatever worked, right?

"Andie, are you done washing?" I heard Luna tentatively call out from behind the fabric door.

Weird. I didn't remember telling her my name.

"Yes, you can come in now." I wrapped the moss towel around myself and watched as she and her mother entered the room. Luna had clothes folded in her hands, and her mother had a strange-looking bag, which she used to put my suit into.

"For later." She motioned toward it but wouldn't say more.

Luna laid out a white tunic and brown belt on the bed for me to change into and handed me a comb made of twigs to brush out my hair. The two of them left the room again, and I changed into the long shirt, putting the belt at my waist. There were no mirrors, so there was no telling how I looked after combing out my wet hair, but honestly, it was the least of my worries.

Grabbing the pack Sola had put my suit into, I pulled the cloth back and peeked into the other room. Luna and Sola stood on either side of the doorway, facing the front of the home. At that same moment, two young fairy boys whizzed in through the central door carrying trays laden with food. They set the large trays on a low table surrounded by floor pillows. Backing away, they stood on either side of the main door facing us, with arms behind their backs and their eyes staring straight forward.

I was getting a serious "army" vibe from some of these fairies. What was going on with them?

Jasper chose that moment to land inside the home, his ugly troll face clean and his dirty clothes gone. But the sneer and evil beady eyes were the same.

"I see you're all ready to go!" He clapped his hands together in glee. I knew he had plans for me, and it worried me. I struggled to stay in place and not approach him. My hands itched to strangle his scrawny neck. I had a sense that if I did, I would ruin whatever Luna and Sola had planned.

"First, before we go, you must eat a good meal." He gestured toward the food, and I moved around the table to seat myself on one of the pillows farthest from him. The food before me was strange, and I had no idea what any of it was. I was hesitant to try any of it.

In front of me, there was a plate with small purple things that resembled biscuits. Green slabs of something resembling meat lined another plate, and various other strange colored foods graced other trays. The only thing that looked vaguely familiar was white button mushrooms lying atop a green lettuce-like leaf.

Luna, who had sat down beside me, leaned over while Jasper turned to confer with one of the fairy boys. "Berry biscuits, toad steak, mushroom salad, sugar snaps, and rose nectar," she said, gesturing to each one.

Toad steak was out of the question. I didn't care how hungry I was—that was not and nor would never be appealing to me. Sola handed me a small plate, and I placed a berry biscuit, mushroom salad, and some sugar snaps on it. Luna passed me a glass of rose nectar. I nibbled on the biscuit and found it to be surprisingly good. Sweet and tart with the buttery flavor of a biscuit. The mushroom salad was okay, but not flavorful. It had more of an earthy flavor, and I didn't take another bite. The sugar snaps reminded me of sugar cookies, but much lighter and airier. I tried a sip of the rose nectar and found it tasted like flavored flower water. Big surprise, right? I'd rather just drink plain water.

I ate fast, even though I wasn't very hungry. I just wanted to get the meal over with so that we could get on with whatever was to happen. I knew my body needed sustenance, though. Luna and Sola ate calmly beside me while Jasper finished talking with the young fairies. They promptly took flight after he dismissed them.

Turning back to us, he grinned and hurried over, the look in his eyes diabolical. "I see you've finished up, so now it is time to go. Luna will accompany us."

He walked behind me, reaching down, his hands grabbing me under my arms as he pulled me up from the pillow. I couldn't help myself and had to swat his vile hands away, jumping to face him.

"*Don't* touch me!" I yelled. The words exploding from me in anger before I caught myself. His face turned a mottled red, and his eyes bulged. Biting my lip, I knew I'd made a terrible mistake.

"Well, we could have done this the easy way, little girl, but you've just made it a lot more difficult for yourself—and a lot more enjoyable for me! Luna, get the ties!"

"But Jasper, do we truly need to use it? She can't fly, and she doesn't know where we are going," Luna said.

I was immediately on alert.

He held his hand up, shaking his head, signaling for her to stop talking. She promptly bowed her head and turned to a cabinet, opening it and pulling out something that looked like black rope.

"Don't just stand there. Tie her hands up so we can be on our way!" Jasper paced back and forth in front of me, agitated and impatient.

Luna lightly brought my hands behind me, looping the rope around them. "I'm sorry," she whispered as the rope she had let go of tightened on its own around my wrists so securely that I could feel it biting into my skin as if it had teeth. Warmth oozed down my hands.

I breathed through the pain. I knew I had to, or Jasper would most likely go ballistic. The sooner we were on our way, the faster this torture would end.

Jasper saw that I was all taken care of, and we said our goodbyes to Sola as Jasper took flight. Luna wrapped her arms around me, taking off after him. We soared through the trees and up through the hole in the cave's roof. The air outside was crisp, and I shivered as the wind hit my bare legs. Jasper glanced back to make sure we were following as he darted in and out of the tall trees. The moon was the only light as we flew.

This time was not as fun as the first time had been. My wrists were burning behind me, the cold seeped into my bones, and I was dreading whatever we were flying into. I wanted to ask Luna so many questions, but it scared me that Jasper might overhear us.

As we glided closer to a field, I heard voices below us, and I strained to see who it was. We flew straight over the opening in the forest, and then I saw them.

It's the guys!

I didn't think first but yelled as emphatically as I could. "Guys! I'm here! Look up! Please help me!"

No one looked up, and Luna clapped her hand over my mouth, keeping me from screaming out again. I looked up to see Jasper tearing through the sky toward us, fury in his eyes.

"You witch!! *Shut up*! You will ruin it for us all. They can't hear you, anyway! Your voice is too small, and we are too high up. Freya will owe me big after this. You're way more trouble than I could have expected. We are almost there. Now behave yourself, or you won't appreciate the consequences." He snarled as he swung back to continue the journey.

My heart thumped unevenly, and I felt ill, knowing my friends were down there. I knew in my bones that they would have done anything they could to help me if they had only heard me.

Wait! Charlie!!

Charlie was supposed to scout and let the group know if anything was approaching them. Could he have seen us and alerted the rest of the guys? Oh, please, please let him have done so! I held on to that hope as we began to descend lower into the forest, and I could see the roof of a cottage below us, gray smoke curling out of the chimney.

As we flew closer, the home got bigger. Jasper darted into a window that had been left cracked open, and I remembered that we were smaller, the size of dragonflies. I had to figure out a way to get bigger, or I would never be able to get away.

Luna and I followed through the window into a dank, cold room. The furniture lay broken inside, layers of dust covered every surface. We continued through a busted door into a hallway littered with dirt and leaves. Closed doors lined the hall. Something about this place seemed familiar somehow.

A glow flickered from a larger room ahead, and Jasper zipped around the corner impatiently. "Why are you going so slow, Luna? We don't have all day!" he hissed.

Luna didn't increase her speed as he turned back to the room, and I worked on gathering my courage, reminding myself that I had powers—at least I thought I still did. Luna grasped one of my hands and placed a tiny ball into it, curling my fingers around it, and whispered into my ear.

"When your hands are free, you must eat it at once. It will reverse the spell so that you can go back to normal size. Remember, not all of us are like Jasper."

We rounded the corner into a dimly lit room on the heels of her last words.

A few candles flickered on nearby tables, and a crackling fire put out a peaty smell. In front of the fire stood a woman with her back to us. Her black hair curled down her back, and she wore a long black dress. I sensed power emanating from her all the way across the room, and I was vaguely aware of others standing in the shadows watching.

It was Freya.

"I've been waiting for you, Andie." She casually turned around. She was the same crazy woman from the diner. Only now, her eyes glowed with amber light, and evil almost dripped from her skin.

She motioned for Luna to bring me closer as Jasper landed on her shoulder, smug and self-righteous. Freya scrutinized me as Luna held me, and the sheer size of her in front of us overwhelmed me.

"Jasper, I commend you for your efforts. You will be repaid handsomely for your loyalty to our cause. Take her bindings off. She is no threat to me like this, and the Fomori won't be able to keep her in one piece if they continue to smell her blood." She grinned like something was funny, and Jasper joined in.

Fury welled up inside my chest, and I wished with all my might that I was my average size so that I could scratch the hateful smile off her face. I wouldn't stand a chance, though, if the Fomori were here with her. It didn't surprise me since she was working with them. All of Hunter's stories of his childhood came surging into my thoughts, making my blood boil further.

Luna uttered a few words I couldn't understand, and the bindings loosened and dropped to the floor. Stretching my arms out beside me, I eased the stiffness that had set in while they were tied up. I kept my hands fisted so that the ball Luna gave me didn't fall out. I needed it, and soon.

Luna sat me down smoothly on the floor and then immediately flew behind me. Freya and Jasper were too busy arguing about his reward to pay any attention to my actions, so I promptly popped the ball into my mouth and swallowed. A bitter taste filled my mouth, like pickles and oranges mixed together, and pressure began building. I hoped the antidote didn't cause me to get ill as I had before. I didn't have time for it, and I'd never get out of this place if it did.

Energy pulsed around me, and Freya snapped her head around in my direction as my joints popped. I was growing fast. There was some pain, but nothing like I had dreaded. Luna screeched a spell behind me, and the bag with my suit landed at my side. It had been enlarged as well. I sensed the Fomori coming out of their hiding spots while Freya lunged for me. My body was almost its normal size, and the tunic I had been wearing had long since been reduced to tatters.

Turning, I ran naked back down the hall we had come from, flinging my suit free from the bag as I ran. I knew I didn't have time to stop and put it on. The last door in the hall loomed in front of me, and I flung myself through it, slamming it behind me as I chanted.

Where there were clothes, now there are none.
Place this suit on me, my will be done.

I put every flickering bit of energy into the words, and within moments the purple suit hugged my body again. I didn't have time to celebrate this win as I heard footsteps marching down the hall.

Looking up to take in the room and search for a way out, I was immediately hit with a rotten egg stench, and my mouth opened in horror. *The vision from my dream.* Body parts scattered around the room. Blood and gore splashed the walls. My eyes searched out the corners for the horned creature. There was no one there. Relief overcame me while the door flung open, urging me out of a frozen stupor.

My heart stopped cold when my legs wouldn't move, no matter how much I willed them to.

"It seems that Andie needs to be shown a lesson." Freya's voice dripped with anger and excitement. "I think she needs to understand what her people are up against, and what happens when someone thinks that they can beat me. I'd like to see how she feels about our friends. Then she might tell us where the treasures are."

Some magical force compelled me to look at Freya standing in the doorway. She motioned to the shadows in the hall behind her, and two hellish creatures stepped out of the darkness as she moved to the side.

My heart pounded so powerfully that I heard it in my ears, and I bit my tongue to keep from yelling in horror. Both creatures looked exactly like the one that had been waiting in the corner of the bloody room in my dream. Evil grins spread across their grotesque faces as they drifted closer, smelling the air, and I suppose my blood.

"Don't be rude. Say hello to my friends, you impertinent child!" Freya laughed evilly as she studied the fear in my eyes. I stuttered but couldn't seem to form words. "No? Well, don't worry. They'll hear you scream soon enough."

Turning back toward the hall as if she had no interest in me anymore, she waved her arms into the air and the Fomori were on me in the next instant.

I must not scream. I must not scream!

The mantra went through my mind over and over as they walked behind me. They licked the blood off my wrists, and the sickening feeling soon turned to scalding as one bit into the already open wound to widen the sore. I squeezed my eyes shut, biting the inside of my cheek until blood welled.

Suddenly the two stopped laving at my skin and walked around in front of me, mirroring each other's steps. They looked me up and down, both holding small knives that looked like scalpels. Neither said a word, which was frightening because they didn't give away what was coming.

Freya still faced the dark hall; I didn't think she had moved an inch. Both Fomori reached out, cutting into my feet. Small cuts that weren't deep, but enough to cause dark red blood to well. Over and over they made these cuts on every part of my exposed body. In between cutting, they would lick the blood, and guttural noises from them soon echoed in the room as they grew into a frenzy. My body was on fire from all the little cuts, and even though blood was not pouring from me, I worried about blood loss, and that they would soon tear me apart.

At some point, I managed to distance myself from what was happening, focusing on my friends and their faces in my mind. That was until the monsters started cutting my face, and the pain was finally too much to bear. I let myself slip into oblivion.

Sometime later, I awoke on the dirty wood floor. Body parts and blood surrounded me, and I fought to keep the bile down. My head swam from the blood I had lost, but I tried to focus on every part of the room. *Where were they? Was this a trick?*

Raised voices came from another part of the house. Jasper was screaming Luna's name. Did she help get them away from me? I could only guess that she did, but I didn't want it to be in vain.

Spotting a window across the room, and with no thought but getting out, I barreled toward it, flinging my body through as hard as I could. Glass shattered around me, and slivers stuck to my skin as I tumbled to the ground outside. Tucking my head into my arms to protect it as best I could from the hard fall, I rolled.

Shouting sounded from the edge of the forest, and Freya roared from inside the house. I didn't want to witness her anger again. Cuts all over my body were nothing compared to what I knew she could have the Fomori do. Rolling to my feet, I ran toward the voices near the trees, praying it wasn't more Fomori.

"Andie!" a voice called out, and Killian rushed out of the trees with Hunter, Teagan, and Emric hot on his heels.

"We don't have time. We have to get out of here now. Freya and Fomori are in there. Oh my God! Luna is in there too! We have to get her—she saved my life!" I panted, realizing that the fairy could be in danger. Turning back to run toward the house, a small hand smacked me in the forehead.

"I'm just fine, thank you. But you won't be if we don't hurry! I can't promise I can save you again. Come on!"

Chapter Fourteen

We tore through the trees, pushing branches out of the way and leaping over logs and small boulders. My breath came fast and heavy. Fear consumed me. Emric ran beside me as the others ran ahead, his tail bouncing as he ran.

"Emric, where's Charlie?" I gasped as my chest burned from the exertion. I never said I was a runner, and nothing could prove it more than how I felt right now.

"He is leading your arch-nemesis on a wild goose chase back there." He chuckled. "We'll be long gone before they figure out that they're not actually chasing you."

Genius. Charlie is pure genius!

"Remind me to get him some bird treats, or whatever it is that he loves to eat. He's simply brilliant." I chuckled at the picture of Freya running after the wrong Andie.

It felt as if we were running for hours. I was exhausted, but I would push myself as much as I possibly could to get far away from the evil I had witnessed. I still didn't know who the victims of the Fomori back in that house were, but the picture of that room was seared into my mind, making me shudder.

The trees began to thin out, and I noticed something etched onto several of the tree trunks that we passed by. Paying closer attention, I saw that it was the symbol of the treasures. I couldn't take my eyes off them, shocked that this was another one of my dream scenes, except nothing was hot on my heels. Aine was right; I had been foreseeing the future.

"*Oomph*!"

I bounced to the ground, landing hard on my butt, my teeth jarred from the impact. Dazed, I looked up to see Hunter staring down at me with a searing look. I stared back, suddenly shy due to the way we had parted before. I wasn't sure if he was still angry with me or not.

I could see Teagan and Killian behind him, watching us. Teagan looked uncomfortable, and Killian looked bored while Luna found a spot on his head to perch.

"You just can't help running into me, can you, short stack?"

Hunter smirked, but his eyes showed relief as he reached down to pull me up from the ground, straight into his arms. He wrapped me in a tight hug, and his heart thumped rapidly in his chest. He smelled of wood smoke and cedarwood. Pushing his face into my hair, he took a deep breath in.

"Don't leave us again, Andie. We were so worried," he said quietly, but I could hear his voice tremble before he abruptly sat me back from him. Teagan and Killian came over, and each gave me a careful hug, smiling and asking if I was okay.

"Yes, I'm so much better now. The only real damage I sustained were the cuts from the glass in the window, these cuts on my face, and this..." I held out my wrists that were still slightly oozing blood from the binds that had cut into me.

In the background, Luna explained to Killian about the magical rope and how she had to bind me, while Teagan looked the sore spots over. Killian peppered her with questions, his favorite thing to do, yet she didn't seem to mind at all and animatedly explained all that had happened.

"Okay, Andie, we're going to heal them, but I'm afraid it's still going to leave a scar."

"It's okay, Teagan. I'll use any scars I get as reminders that next time I need to fight harder and be stronger. "He nodded and gently laid his palms over the striations, whispering a spell that caused his hands to glow. Heat flowed into my wrists, and I watched in fascination as my skin knitted itself back together slowly. When he was done, all that remained was a slightly raised pink line that went around each wrist.

"Look, I've got permanent bracelets!" I joked. They all just shook their heads and turned away to get their packs to head back out. Emric chuckled as he rubbed against my leg.

At least he thought I was funny.

Looking back down at the lines on my wrists, I noticed a soft green glow coming from the dragonfly that circled my forearm. Excitement bubbled in my chest at the sight.

"Uh, guys, does this mean what I think it does?" I showed them my bracelet, and Luna flew off Killian's head to see it better.

"Wow! I've only seen one of those once before, and it was owned by Coeus. Please tell me—did he give that to you?" She seemed thrilled by the thought, and I verified that he had, explaining how it was supposed to light up brighter the closer we got to the first Key.

She sighed in relief. "That bracelet does more than you know. You are very lucky to have it. *We* are very lucky that you do."

"Wait a second, Luna... You know Coeus?"

Her bright green eyes lost some of their sparkle, and she looked down at her clasped hands, fidgeting and nodding.

"I do. My mother and I both do. We are his descendants. I know when you look at me now, you only see a fairy. But once, we were like you, not tiny and winged. A spell was placed upon us, much like the one that was forced on you by the candlewig flower. Except ours has no antidote that we know of. You may have noticed slight differences between us and the other fairies. We were sold to Jasper, and he's been using us to gather more slaves, much the same way you were taken. Most of the fairies you saw working for him were once like you. They were lured to the cave and changed forever. It's all part of Freya and the Fomori's plan to try and grow their army. My mother and I began our plot to escape when we heard the plans for you. Mother made the antidote, and we knew I would need to be the one to get you away from Freya's clutches."

My mind whirled with what she was saying. "But Luna, who did that to you, and why?"

"It was Asteria. She is the daughter of Coeus, the Goddess of Falling Stars and Necromancy. She thought that my mother and I were trying to take her favored place in her father's eyes. Never would we have wanted that or done that. We were only friends of his, nothing more, nothing less. But Asteria went mad with jealousy and twisted everything in her mind. Where once she was good, she soon turned to evil. She made it her mission to strip us from his life, and she succeeded."

I watched in silence as she took off toward the trees, obviously wanting to be alone. I vowed to myself that I would try to find a way to help her and her mother, as they had helped me. It might not be anytime soon, but I would add it to my list of to-dos.

Turning to face the rest of the group, I wiped my sweaty hands on my suit. When I did, I felt a lump in one of the many pockets that lined my legs. I didn't remember putting anything in it, though. Worried about what I might find, I gingerly opened it and reached my hand in. Knitted fabric brushed my fingers, and I pulled out my beanie. How had I forgotten about it? I then realized that I hadn't worn it since we had crossed through the first portal. With everything going on, I hadn't even given it a thought. Elation at something familiar spread through me, and I slapped it on my head, tugging it down over my ears.

"Uh, Andie?" Teagan looked at me, his eyes wide, and I saw that Hunter and Killian wore similar expressions.

"What is it? Please don't tell me there's a monster standing behind me. I really, really don't want you to tell me that," I whispered.

"No, there's no monster behind you. But, um, we can't see you. You disappeared. Which can't be right because we can hear you," Killian supplied.

I scoffed. "What do you mean I disappeared? I'm standing right here!" I pointed at the ground, but none of them noticed. Looking down, I stumbled a bit when I didn't see my shoes or my legs.

"Whoa." This was so weird. Dread came then. What had happened?

Killian walked up to where I was standing, both of his hands straight out in front of him until one of them smacked right into my nose.

"Ouch! Watch it! That really hurt, Killian!" I backed away from him, and he looked embarrassed, his cheeks stained bright red.

"Sorry, Andie! I just figured if I couldn't see you, you were like a ghost or something, and my hand would go right through you. I swear I didn't mean to hit you."

Sighing, I took off my beanie, running my hands through my hair, trying to figure out what had happened and how to fix it.

"Hey, shorty, you're back," Hunter stated nonchalantly like this happened every day. I looked at my hands, and sure enough, I could see them again, and my blue beanie in my fist.

"Guys. How is this possible? I think it was my beanie! I put it on, and then the next thing I know, I'm invisible. Then I just took it off, and now you can see me again!"

This was my mother's beanie, had she somehow spelled it to work in a Fae world? It had never made me invisible before. Incredible! I could imagine all the ways that this would come in handy during our journey.

"Where did that beanie come from?" Teagan asked as he reached for it, his eyes questioning if it was okay to take it. I grudgingly handed it over, his hand gently brushing against mine as I watched him take the beanie with the utmost care. I got the feeling he could tell it meant a lot to me.

"It was my mother's. I found it when I was young, and it's the only thing I have of hers. I can't believe it's magic." I breathed, staring at the blue yarn.

Teagan ran his hand over it, and I could tell he was concentrating, seeing something in it that I hadn't. When he was done, he handed it back over to me. "Your mother definitely spelled this. I can feel a magical imprint on it similar to yours. She must have had a reason. It would only have activated like the spell your nan had put on you when you crossed over to Fae." He smiled as he turned away, and I could see the thoughtful looks on Hunter and Teagan's faces as well.

Even though she wasn't here, she was somehow taking care of me in this small way. My heart warmed as I hugged the beanie to my chest before tucking it away in the pocket again.

"One is always watching out for who they love, even if they are no longer around..." Emric purred as he wound around my legs. I realized he was righter than he knew.

We began our travels again through the forest, knowing that we needed to put as much distance between ourselves and Freya as we could. After Charlie had his fun with them, Freya would be in a foul mood.

As we walked, the bracelet pulsed with green light, reassuring me that we were still on the right path. I relayed what had transpired since I had left them, including the white fox and how I felt like it had been Freya leading me to the cave. Charlie soon rejoined us and confirmed that he had bought us some time, but that Freya and the Fomori weren't far behind.

After hours of walking, and when the light started to wane, we came upon a rickety shed that had been abandoned. It wasn't big, and the door had fallen off the hinges, but at least it gave us somewhere to hunker down for the night. We were exhausted and needed to rest for the coming days. The air was cooler now that the surrounding forest had grown less dense, and the wind whistled through the branches. I swear it carried the smell of seawater.

Killian and Teagan settled in against the walls of the small shack, and Emric curled up beside them. Luna stretched out on his back after zipping in from wherever she had been. She pulled his tail up to cover her like a blanket and was soon asleep.

Teagan began a small magical fire on the floor in front of us, and I felt some relief at the warmth, while Killian brought out the last of our meager food supply. He passed small pieces of jerky around to us, and we chewed it slowly, savoring every bite. Hunter took his and walked back out to sit down beside the broken door. He obviously planned to keep watch for us tonight, and I was grateful. I trusted him to protect us while we were vulnerable.

It felt as if I hadn't slept in weeks, and my suit and the fire were keeping me cozy and warm. Teagan's shoulder rested beside mine as I slipped in between him and Killian, leaning my head back against the wooden walls and closing my eyes on a sigh. I felt myself drifting off, and a hand brushed the hair from my face as my head slid down onto Teagan's shoulder. I snuggled closer as the world drifted away.

Everything burned! My body was on fire, and I could see flames as they licked at my limbs, sizzling against my skin. A huge snake lay in the fire in front of me, its serpent tongue flicking out to lash against the side of my cheek like a whip exacerbating the burning of the fire. The pain was more than I could take, and I screamed and screamed.

"Andie! It's just a dream! Shhh... Wake up, Andie!"

The piercing screams died from my mouth, and I gasped, my eyes flying open. I was cradled in Teagan's warm arms; no longer was the burning consuming me. Tears leaked from the corners of my eyes as I looked up into his concerned face. His hand smoothed my hair as he rocked me back and forth. Sniffling, I wiped my nose, turning my face into his chest. I was so sick of these visions. I just wanted a good night's sleep, and I wished more than anything that I had my music here with me now.

"I'm sorry for waking everyone up," I mumbled into the front of his suit. Embarrassed and upset all at the same time. I didn't want to burn or be in a situation where I could be burned. The memory from it was horrific. Comfort that the past visions hadn't ended up the same in real life was all that I had to hang onto. Realistically though, I knew that it was the actions of others that helped keep them from becoming real.

"Andie, you've slept forever. I was even able to get a nap in after Killian woke up. Don't worry about us. We're okay. It's you we're concerned about." Hunter loomed in the doorway, Killian by his side. Concern made his eyebrows lower as he looked at Teagan and me.

His worry warmed me considerably. Our group had grown close during our journey and I knew that they would do anything to help me. Taking a deep breath, I rested my head back on Teagan's chest and looked at them all. Hunter's gaze changed from concern to something else as he watched me snuggle in Teagan's arms.

Was that jealousy?

I continued to watch Hunter until he felt my gaze on him. His eyes slid to mine, and he schooled his features into a blank look before wiping his hand across his face and shaking his head.

Teagan patted my shoulder. "Let's get you up. We need to get moving as soon as you are ready. Charlie says they're nearly halfway here already."

I looked around at everyone else, watching as they began to pack up their things. As much as I'd like to procrastinate, I knew we had to hurry and find the first treasure. With Freya on our heels, if I didn't get it soon, this entire journey would be all for nothing.

With me dead, Freya would find the treasures eventually and destroy everything and everyone we were trying to protect.

Standing up, I brushed through my tangled hair with my fingers as best I could, stretched, and dusted myself off. Reaching a hand down to Teagan, I looked into his deep gray eyes, then took in the rest of our crew. They were all ready and waiting to do whatever was needed. No matter that we faced many dangers, or that they might be hurt or worse. I was so proud of our band of misfits. All of us different, but all of us ready to do what was right and what was scary to find this first treasure.

I smiled at them, hoping they saw in my face how much I appreciated each and every one of them. I couldn't do this alone—I knew that now.

"Let's do this!"

Chapter Fifteen

The sun peeked over the horizon, and the sky above was clear, a faint breeze ruffled through the leaves as we got started. Breathing in deeply, the crisp morning air filled my lungs, and I felt a strange calm even with the uncertainty of what today or tomorrow would bring.

Charlie soared above, keeping an eye out for anything ahead or behind us, which reassured me as we started today's journey. No longer on any sort of path, we trudged through the trees and tropical flowers. Their fragrance wafted through the air, sweet and heavy. Our whole team seemed to be in a lighter mood today, even the usually surly Hunter.

Teagan led us, making sure to push away any branches in our way, and Emric pounced behind me. I looked back to see him playing with some sort of seed pod that was the shape of a ball. His mouth curved in a hilarious grin. Hunter walked behind him, stutter-stepping a few times to keep from running into the silly Phooka. He rolled his eyes, but they danced with mirth as he grinned back at me.

Turning back to the rest of the group, Killian was skipping behind Teagan while Luna flew circles around his head. She was singing a strange, melodic song as she twirled her hands above her head, wings daintily fluttering behind her.

Part of me knew something strange was happening, but I laughed it off, chalking it up to a good morning and that everyone was happy.

Emric joined in with Luna, adding a funny accent to the song. *Was that Irish?*

I giggled behind my hand and felt a little extra bounce to my step as we continued. Purple flowers become abundant in the next few minutes of our walk, obscuring all of the green plants we had seen before. They weren't large, but the stalks had to be at least five feet tall, with bell-shaped flowers growing up the entire length of each stem. The purple petals drooped down like bells.

That's it! Bluebells!

Their scent became heady as we looked around in fascination. Emric and Luna's song picked up intensity, and our feet began tapping and moving a little faster.

Killian laughed, running from his spot ahead of me, his arm outstretched, hitting all the flowers as he ran by, scattering pollen into the air above us. It floated in slow motion through the air, the yellow puffs triggering a memory in my mind. I felt the wide grin on my face falling.

Something wasn't right here.

Looking back, I saw Hunter running next to Killian, both swatting at the flowers and sending more plumes into the air, a maniacal look glittered in both of their eyes.

Coldness gripped me as I stared at them. Emric and Teagan rolled around in the dust, laughing and playing. Luna had wandered off, but I could still hear her singing from somewhere nearby.

I had to do something! Either the pollen was doing this, or someone had set a trap to keep us from our mission. Tiptoeing over to Hunter, I shook him as hard as I could. He just swept me up in his arms and started dancing around. *What the heck?* I began to feel a tug of mirth in my chest again but tamped it down. I had to use all my will power and grit my teeth to resist the strong pull of it.

Ugh. This would be so much fun if we didn't have a group of people on their way to kill us!

I hated doing this, but I slapped Hunter across the face as hard as I could. Red bloomed on his cheek, and he faltered. I could see his eyes clearing, the realization of what was going on swept across his face, but his body didn't stop dancing.

Think! Think! I had to do something different!

The pollen now coated us, and everything around us was a bright fuzzy yellow. The only thing I could think to do was to try my Fae magic and hope it worked. It wouldn't be good if it backfired. I hadn't tried using it very much; I was still very much a newbie. Oh well! Here goes nothing! I thought of the words to use in my rhyme and crossed my fingers and toes.

Pollen flying, and pollen bright,
Keep the pollen from taking flight.
Happy, dancing, out of control,
Return my friends to their normal souls.
Stop this madness, right away!
Put it back from which it came!

I focused all my energy on the words I was saying, pushing it out through my palms. Power rippled through the air, hitting each of my friends with a jolt, causing them all to fall to the ground. I caught myself when I slipped out of Hunter's arms as he went down. I reached to cradle his head to protect it from hitting the ground.

To the left, Luna slipped out of one of the bluebells like a wet noodle, landing on the ground with a soft thump. I winced, hoping that she wasn't hurt.

No one moved at all, and I panicked. Their eyes were closed, and I couldn't tell if they were breathing. Bending down to Hunter, I put my hand in front of his nose to feel if there was any air coming out. His eyes snapped open as I did, and the yellow glow of his wolf eyes glinted back at me.

I leaned back fast with my hands in the air. "Whoa!"

He blinked a few times, and his eyes returned to their normal shade of warm coffee brown; however, they were clouded with confusion. In the background, I could hear the rest of our group groaning and getting up around us.

"Andie? What happened?" Hunter asked as he sat up.

"Honestly? I have no idea. We were walking, and then suddenly, we all, myself included, started acting weird. We were singing and dancing, totally out of control. I tried to snap you out of it, and well, it didn't work out so well. Sorry about your cheek, by the way." I sucked in a breath at the perfect outline of my hand that still showed an angry red.

"I, um, wasn't sure how hard I needed to hit you to snap you out of it. It seemed like it helped at first, but then whatever it was took over again. You kinda picked me up and danced around with me. I couldn't get away, so the only other thing I could think of to do was a spell. Thankfully it worked!"

Emric pawed the pollen near him and blew out a deep breath, scattering the rest of the yellow fuzz away from him.

"It was sprites. Wood sprites, to be exact. They enjoy playing tricks when one enters their territory. Bluebells aren't poisonous, but the sprites have spelled the pollen, and I'm quite sure they have probably enjoyed a grand ole show, they did!" He harrumphed before yelling into the mass of flowers, "You hear me, you wee buggers? If I had more time, I'd come in there and eat you all!"

I raised my eyebrows at Teagan, only to have him shrug his shoulders and nod grimly at me. I knew Emric could be dangerous, but I didn't want to imagine him eating small creatures that might be harmless other than their pranks. I wouldn't want to be on the other end of his anger.

We tried to dust the sticky pollen from our clothes and hair, but it was next to impossible. It clung to every inch of us like super glue. We would just have to try and find a stream or some other body of water to wash off in soon.

Charlie chose that moment to soar above us in his black raven form, screeching repeatedly as he descended before landing lightly on my shoulder. Emric jumped up from his spot on the ground, and his body immediately changed to panther form. It happened so fast that it made my head spin.

"Freya and her army are almost on us," he ground out.

Everyone jumped into motion. Grabbing our packs, we darted out of the flowers, running faster than ever. Our lives depended on it. Luna and Charlie flew ahead since we now knew what was behind us. I was frightened, but I was determined to either lose Freya and the Fomori or outrun them.

As we ran, there were rustling noises in the flowers that surrounded us. Startled, I saw hundreds of small stick-like figures hopping from flower to flower beside us as we ran. Twigs stuck up from the top of their heads, their version of hair, I guess. Little human-like faces stared back at us, and they all chanted in unison, their eyes glowing purple.

"Teagan, do something!" I yelled up to him. "I don't know what they're saying but it sounds like a spell. I don't have the patience to break another one right now!"

I panted with the exertion as I leapt over a large rock, and Emric lashed out at some of the sprites closest to him, scattering them back into the flowers. Teagan called back to me from the front of the group. "Okay, but I'm going to need some of your power to help me, Andie. You need to focus on pushing it to me when you hear me begin saying the spell.

"Got it!" I yelled back.

Looking behind me, I saw Hunter reach out to grab a particularly annoying sprite that was keeping pace with him, sticking its little wooden tongue out at him and laughing. Every time Hunter reached for it, the creature would dance backward, somehow thwarting his attempts and making him more aggravated.

I felt the air begin to shift around us and knew that Teagan was starting the spell. I could see a faint white light surrounding him, and he shouted the spell. That was strange... I'd never seen any color around him before.

I concentrated on pulling magic to me and pushing it out toward the glowing aura that outlined Teagan. As I did, the white light grew bigger and brighter. When he finished the spell, he threw the bubble of power outward, and sparkles exploded over the sprites running beside us. I braced myself. Would they explode or something equally startling? Instead, to my amazement, all the wood sprites began to float into the air, frozen and unable to move. Thousands rose out of the bluebells, and the sparkles from the spell surrounded them. It was surreal.

"No time to gawk, shorty. We have to get going." Hunter nudged me, and I realized I had stopped running. That was such a cool spell! I'd have to remind Teagan to teach it to me later. I only hoped that they weren't hurt or in pain. They looked peaceful, though.

"Don't worry, Andie!" Teagan called, still running. "In ten minutes or so, they'll be back to normal!"

Relieved, I took a deep breath and sprinted after them. I only hoped that the sprites would cause just as much trouble or more for Freya. I just worried that she wouldn't be as kind to them as Teagan had.

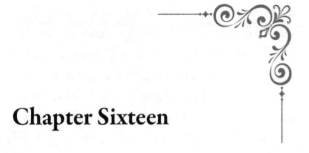

Chapter Sixteen

S weat dripped onto my eyebrows as we ran at a full speed. My pack bounced against my back, and my legs ached. This time Hunter led us while Teagan ran behind me, neither looking winded at all. Whenever we made it back home, I was going to have to join a gym and get into better shape. I still needed Hunter to teach me how to be a good fighter.

The air was gradually turning from crisp and cool to humid and warm. The trees and tropical plants beginning to thin out the further we ran, and the ground was softer. Looking down, I saw shells scattered in the brown dirt that looked to be mixed with white sand. Somewhere in the distance, there was the soft swooshing of water.

"I think we must be near an ocean or lake!" Teagan exclaimed just as Hunter stopped suddenly, throwing his arms out wide. We crowded beside him, peering around to see what the issue was.

In front of us, a massive gorge stretched as far as we could see in the fog that hung low around it. A rickety-looking rope bridge stretched out into the dense cloud, preventing us from being able to see the end of the bridge and what was on the other side.

"Where does that bridge lead, Hunter? Can you smell anything? Do your wolf senses give you the vision to see through the fog?" Killian pummeled Hunter with question after question, and I pictured smoke coming out of his ears like they do in cartoons.

He huffed out a breath, not even looking at Killian, who was practically glued to his side. "I don't know where it goes. I smell seawater, and no, my eyes don't give me x-ray vision, fog vision or future vision," he deadpanned. "All I have is superior night vision."

Emric snickered as he wound between us, hopping onto the bridge and then confidently sashaying across it, while Charlie flew ahead into the fog. The rest of us looked at each other. All our faces showed uncertainty at the thought of crossing this dangerous bridge, especially when we didn't know what was on the other side. Surely Charlie would warn us if any danger was ahead.

Well, someone had to make a move, so who better than me? Regardless of the mental images I had of falling off this death trap, I took a deep breath and charged ahead. Hunter and Teagan protested when they saw me move, both thinking that they should go first.

I knew I needed to do this. Not just to prove to myself that I could, but to show them that I could lead and push forward when I needed to.

I gave them both a stern look, and they clamped their mouths shut mid-sentence, cutting off excuses why a big bad boy should go before me. There was a light touch on my shoulder as I grabbed ahold of the rough brown rope on either side, and I turned to see Luna sitting there. Guess she wasn't keen on the idea of flying into the fog alone.

"We'll do this together," she firmly stated.

I nodded once, taking a deep breath, and gingerly stepped onto the ropes forming a crisscrossed path underneath my feet. I had to be careful that I didn't lose my footing and slip through one of the openings.

Slowly, I stepped forward, and the bridge immediately began to sway from side to side. I gulped, worried that it might come apart under my weight. That alone made me want to hurry across it, but I knew that wouldn't be a smart decision.

"Guys, I think we should have each of you wait to get on until one of us is at least fifty feet away. This thing is swaying pretty bad already, and I'm not sure how much weight it can take at one time. I'd rather not find out. I'll call out to you after I take fifty steps."

"Andie, if anything happens or you need us, yell right away. I can change to the wolf and get there quick." I glanced back over my shoulder at Hunter and saw the serious and concerned look in his eyes.

"I will." My voice shook slightly. My palms were damp as I gripped the rough rope tightly and took a hesitant step forward, then another. I continued slowly, counting each step and keeping my eyes on the rope below to make sure I didn't step through one of the holes. It comforted me some that I couldn't see anything below or around me. As scared as I was of what might be out there, not knowing might just be better.

It was quiet the further I went. The only sound I could hear was the constant, gentle flow of water coming from somewhere up ahead.

"You're doing good, Andie. Better than I could have expected..." Luna muttered beside my ear. I faltered a little at her strange words. They sounded somewhat encouraging, but the way she said it just didn't seem right. I glanced at her, and her face looked serene, no malice at all. I guess I was imagining things with all the stress I was under. Beginning again, I continued counting until I reached fifty steps.

"Okay, next one up! I'm at fifty steps!" I called back behind me, hoping that the guys could hear me.

I felt the slightest movement as one of them stepped on. Knowing I needed to keep the space between us, I looked down and began the treacherous walk once again. Luna stayed quiet on my shoulder, most likely trying to keep from distracting me, and I was thankful for that. Any misstep could be disastrous.

After counting out another forty steps, I stopped to take my bearings, and I noticed the fog around me was beginning to dissipate. I could see light glinting off something ahead but couldn't quite make out what it was yet. As I strained to see, I began to hear the call of birds somewhere. The noise reminded me of seagulls that would always steal my food when Nan took me to the Gulf for vacation. I knew land had to be somewhere up ahead, and boy was I ready to get to it!

I continued, and before long, I saw what lay ahead. There were only about twenty-five more steps, then the bridge led onto white sand that sparkled from the rays of the bright sun beating down on it. Waves rolled ahead of the sand, and groups of birds swooped and swirled above the water, diving in, disappearing into the dark liquid before bursting out again with strange-looking sea creatures in their beaks. My heart beat fast as I slipped on the rope under my feet in my hurry to get to land.

"Ahh!" I gasped, catching myself against the side of the scratchy rope, my eyes drifting down below it. Fear gripped me as I saw the pit that we had traversed over was full of bones. Some looked to have been from humans, and others from huge creatures.

Straightening, I noticed a cave directly under where the bridge ended, and I knew I couldn't make a sound. I suspected that whatever left all those bones down in the pit lived in that cave. I really hoped the guys stayed quiet on their way over.

Looking at Luna, I put my finger to my lips. She just smirked and nodded. Confused as to why she found this funny, and not understanding why she wasn't concerned, I frowned at her and turned back to finally step off the bridge. My feet sank into the sparkling sand.

I had seen white sand before, but nothing like this. I leaned down to grab a handful. It was soft, and there were bits of what looked like mica in it that shone like diamonds when the sun hit it. While I examined it, Luna jumped off my shoulder and flew off around a rock formation.

Letting the sand drift through my fingers, I looked around, wondering where Charlie and Emric had gone, but I knew if there were any issues, Charlie would have let me know by now. My bracelet glowed on my arm, the green light solid now.

We had to be almost to the treasure! Excitement and anxiety poured over me all at once. I questioned whether I could do this, but I had no choice.

Looking toward the water, I was astounded to see an island rising in the water, far out in the ocean. Blinking to try and clear my eyes, I looked again at the sea. Yep, that was a castle that towered up into the sky. The massive building took up most of the island from what I could tell. Spires rounded high on all sides.

A grunt sounded behind me, and I whirled to see Killian sway as he finished crossing the bridge. He looked positively green. I guess the swaying wasn't kind to his stomach, and he had a touch of motion sickness. My thoughts were confirmed when he doubled over, throwing up what little he had eaten onto the sand beside him. I approached him slowly, afraid that if I ran toward him, it might make his sickness worse. He held up his hand to me as he purged some more before standing up and wiping off his mouth.

"I'm okay... I just really did not like that bridge. And those bones under us? Yeah, that did it. I just need a minute to breathe."

Looking over his shoulder I saw another figure approaching on the bridge. Teagan was looking down at the mouth of the cave. I could see in his eyes that he had come to the same conclusion as I had about it as he hurried off the bridge.

"Andie, Killian, are you both all right?" he asked as he swiped his hand through his hair, the sun making the caramel color brighter than before.

"Yeah, just a little anxious." I waved my arm behind me, and they finally noticed the island. "I'm guessing that is where the first treasure is. The bracelet is fully lit up now." I lifted my arm for them to see.

"Where's everyone else?" Teagan asked, his eyebrows knitted in confusion as he looked around.

"I have no idea. When I got here, I didn't see Charlie or Emric anywhere, and Luna flew off around those rocks." I pointed toward the outcropping, curious about what was on the other side. Before I had a chance to walk around and see, a low rumble sounded from the pit beneath the bridge.

My eyes widened as Hunter flew across the end frantically, his eyes wide but determined. As he hit the last ten feet, a huge, gruesome gray claw reached up, talons ripping through the rope that looked so much like twine in the monster's hand. The bridge reeled side to side as Hunter tried to hang on. There were fear and anger in his eyes, and they flashed yellow as his hands gripped the sides.

I held my hands over my mouth as the claw hit the rope repeatedly. I couldn't see the monster that it belonged to, and I didn't want to. Fear for Hunter choked me, and I couldn't scream if I tried. Killian made as if he were going to go toward Hunter, but Teagan held him back as the claw swiped again at the bridge, striking Hunter so hard that he flew over the side.

I couldn't keep the scream from tearing out. My eyes burned, and my chest felt like it was compressed with pressure.

"No, no, no, *NO!*" I yelled, running over to the edge, not caring that the monster was down there. All I could think about was Hunter. On my hands and knees, I frantically looked down into the pit of bones and saw Hunter being dragged into the cave. I still hadn't seen the monster, but from the way Hunter's body looked as he was pulled into the recesses, he was knocked out or dead. No way would he have gone down without a fight. I racked my brain for a spell, an idea, *anything* to get him out of there.

Laughter sounded behind me, and if it were possible, the fear I felt ratcheted up a notch. It was an evil laugh that I knew well.

Freya.

My stomach dropped to my toes when I turned and saw her standing there, surrounded by Fomori. They looked even more formidable in the sunlight, every grotesque feature visible, evil grins on their pocked faces. Freya looked smug and stood confidently as she faced us, this time wearing a black leather suit with her hair twisted in a knot at the back of her head.

"Oh, Andie, Andie, Andie." She tsked, shaking her head and smiling. "You didn't actually think I would let you get away, did you?" Her eyebrows rose and the smile dropped from her face. "You never had a chance!" she hissed at me.

It was then I noticed that Luna sat on one of her shoulders, and on the other sat Sola. Both waved at me when they saw that I had finally seen them. Anger pulsed like lightning through my veins at the knowledge that they had been in on this all along, betraying our group to Freya and the Fomori.

"How could you, Luna!?" I shouted. "Why even bother pretending you were helping us?" I waved my arms around while Freya laughed at my antics. I had to get my temper under control. I realized that I was playing into their hands.

"I'd say I'm sorry, but I'm not." Luna flew toward me, hovering a few feet in front of my face. "I told you the truth about Coeus and Asteria though if that's any consolation. Asteria did cast us out, but she had a good reason." She shrugged her shoulders and then chanted a few words, Sola doing the same. The air around the two of them changed, oily black smoke wafting around their little bodies, stretching longer and swirling faster until I couldn't see them anymore. Then the inky darkness faded, and there stood a full-sized Luna and Sola in front of us, their wings gone.

"We never had a spell cast on us except the one we placed on ourselves to make you believe our little story. Asteria cast us out when she discovered that we decided to work with the Fomori. We were the Titan's personal spell masters, and well, you can imagine that didn't go over well with Coeus or Asteria." She cackled.

Now some of the things that she had said to me made perfect sense, and I didn't know why I hadn't listened to my intuition. They had led Freya right to us, and Luna most likely kept her updated the entire time on our whereabouts when she would always disappear. Frustration and hurt boiled inside me.

I was certain that they had done something with Emric and Charlie but held onto the hope that the two were still hiding out to help us in some way. We needed all the help we could get. Freya was mighty all by herself, but with the Fomori and the witches? We had our work cut out for us.

I couldn't let them capture me; we were so close to Finias and the treasure. Killian and Teagan crowded beside me as we faced off with Freya and her minions. I knew Luna and Sola had a lot of power on their own, and Freya was extremely powerful as well. Whatever Teagan and I did, we'd have to protect Killian. As far as I knew, he had no powers, although there were times that he didn't seem precisely human, and I hadn't asked him before.

Teagan gathered power beside me, and I was sure that the group in front of us was aware of it as well. He grabbed my hand, and I knew that he wanted me to lend him some of mine like I had before.

"Whatever happens, you have to find a way to get to that island, Andie." He glanced at me and saw the hesitation in my eyes. Shaking his head, I knew he was telling me that I didn't have a choice. I had no idea what kind of chance we had against Freya and the Fomori, but I couldn't let everyone down. It was going to be up to me.

Teagan pushed Killian behind us at the same moment he sent a blast of magic toward Freya. The ripples were visible in the air before the concussion hit her and the Fomori.

Seeing my chance, I grabbed the beanie out of my pocket and put it on, instantly becoming invisible. I ran around the group while they were still down. Out of the corner of my eye, a black figure leaped at one of the Witches, yowling and scratching.

I felt a wave of relief and gave thanks that Emric was all right and able to be here and help us. I only wished that Hunter was here too. Anger grew in my chest and fueled my resolve to be successful.

The sounds of fighting grew distant as I ran to the shoreline. Despair filled me as I looked around and realized that there was no way across it. Glancing back, I saw Teagan locked in a deadly battle with Freya and the Fomori. He was bleeding from various cuts on his face and arms, and I knew that he was wearing down. Emric kept Luna and Sola busy, scratching and biting them, causing deep wounds. The look on his face was fierce as he swiped out, knocking Luna back with more force than seemed possible. As he did, I watched Killian, who didn't seem to care that we had warned him to stay out of the fight. He snuck up behind Sola, raising a small boulder from the pile nearby, and smashed her over the head. She instantly crumpled to the ground, blood trickling from the wound into her hair.

On the ground nearby, Luna struggled to get up after seeing her mother go down. Her face screwed up with hate as she stared at Killian. She screamed and shot a spell at him, flames erupting from her fingers, flying directly at him. He didn't try to move away, even though he clearly saw them coming.

Calmly, he stood still while I watched in shock as the fire parted and flew around him, hitting the rocks behind him before dissipating. It was as if he were protected by an invisible field surrounding him.

He definitely had some sort of powers, and I would ask him all about them later, but for now, I had to figure out a way to Finias.

Turning back to the water, I racked my brain to try and figure out a plan, think of a spell, or something that would get me over there. Nothing came to me, and I felt desperate. I would swim if I had to, but I absolutely didn't want to. There was no telling what kind of creatures were in that water that could kill me.

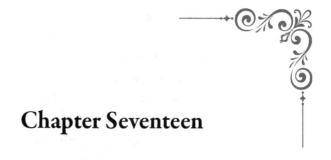

Chapter Seventeen

A sudden gust of wind blew my hair back as a shadow fell over me from above. I grabbed ahold of the beanie to keep it from flying off my head. If Freya saw me, I wouldn't have a chance. Tilting my head back, I looked up at the sky to see what was blocking out the sun.

A winged stag was descending from the air. It had huge antlers that branched from its forehead, and front legs that were hooved. Its back legs were clawed like a falcon's with massive talons that curled, glinting sharply in the sunlight. In place of a tail were long elegant feathers. White wings stretched out on either side of the stag's body, gracefully turning it through the air. I had never seen anything like it before. As it glided closer to me, I could feel that it didn't mean me harm. I didn't know how, but I knew it was true.

With no sound at all, it landed right beside me and looked directly into my eyes. How could it see me when no one else could? As we stared at each other, one of its eyes winked at me, and a deep voice rumbled.

"Helllloooooo, Andie..."

It was Charlie, and I had never been so happy to see him and his ever-changing form.

"Don't worry. They can't hear or see me. Only you can. Hop on, I'm your ride over there!" His deep voice stunned me, and I didn't think twice before grabbing a patch of the scratchy fur on his neck and swinging myself onto his back, relieved that he was okay and that I now had a way to the island.

Wrapping my arms around his neck, I hugged him as he launched into the air, his wings beating against the wind. Before long, we were so high up that the figures below looked like ants, and I couldn't tell who was who. I hoped with all my might that my friends were ok and able to hold Freya off without being hurt badly.

I let myself relax for a moment while we glided through the air, the castle looming ever closer. It had been huge when I saw it from the beach, but now it was gigantic. My bracelet glowed an even brighter green than it had been before, radiating warmth. There was no doubt the treasure was there. I just had no idea what I would be facing to get to it.

One thing was for sure though: I was going to do whatever I needed to get this first Key. My group had been hurt, and maybe worse, to get me here. They didn't question anything, but pushed forward, braving death and injury for me. I had never done anything in my life this important, and I had never had anyone count on me or need me like this. It was an incredible feeling and a terrible feeling all at once. But I would do this for them.

Looking again at the bracelet, the tattoo above it caught my eye. The black lines of the Unalome glittered in the sun, and I thought back to what Aine had told me. I knew that I was transforming with each new experience, and no matter how scared I felt at the unknown, this was a journey I had to take.

We were almost to the castle when Charlie looked back at me in mid-flight. "I'm going to drop you off on the shore, then I have to get back to Emric. He and the others need me."

I could hear the apology in his voice, and I gently patted the side of his head, the rough fur tickling my hand.

"It's okay. I honestly don't want to be alone, but I need you to make sure they're all right. I'll figure all of this out. By the way, what exactly *is* this form that you've taken?"

"A Peryton. It is a demon of the Celestial Corps. They are impervious to all weapons and can play mind games, but not all Perytons are evil just because they are considered demons."

"Good to know..." I wondered how Charlie and Emric decided what to change to. I guessed it depended on the situation.

His head bobbed in acknowledgment before he glided down onto a beach that was strewn with black rock. It was so different from the beautiful white sand from earlier. Sliding off his back, my feet crunched on the rocks as they moved underneath me. I stared in awe at the drawbridge that was lowered over a moat circling around the castle. It was only about five feet away from me, and I thought it was weird that there was one, seeing as how the entire island was covered by the castle, and surrounded by ocean.

Stepping up to the wooden drawbridge, I ran smack into something, my forehead hitting it hard, causing me to bounce backward.

"I forgot to tell you that there is a protection spell around the castle to keep anyone out." Charlie chuckled as he took a leap into the air. "I have all the confidence that you can break it!" His voice echoed as he soared away.

It was deathly quiet here, except for the waves splashing against the rocks. I felt totally alone. Turning, I faced the invisible barrier. I reached out and ran my hand over the shield, studying the energy and magic that weaved through it. I racked my brain for the words that Teagan had used when we went through the mirrored wall in the red flower field.

Quieting my mind, I blocked out the crashing waves and closed my eyes. As I ran my hands over the barrier, the tingling began. Focusing hard, I whispered words that I hoped were correct. I chanted them over and over as the energy in my hands became stronger, and the pinching feeling began. I could feel the barrier pushing back, resisting. This was going to take a lot of power. I reached even deeper inside myself, pulling all the energy that my body would allow.

I WILL not fail! The thought bellowed in my mind.

I screamed with all my might, pushing hard against the force and using all the anger, despair, anxiety, and worry that I had bottled up inside. For Hunter, for my friends and for me, I would get through this.

The resistance in the wall began to falter, and I felt it slide down, my hands pushing right through it. Exhausted from the exertion, I took a moment to catch my breath and still the beating of my heart. Squatting down, I rested my head in my hands, resting both on my knees.

I did it!!

Mentally, I tried to pump myself back up because this was far from over.

I approached the drawbridge with cautious steps. Heavy black chains attached it to the top of the castle, and spikes hung down from the opening. I shuddered to think of them falling on some unsuspecting visitors. The wooden planks on the bridge creaked as I shuffled across, eyeballing those spikes to make sure they weren't going to fall on me as I passed through the opening.

Once through, I let out the breath I had been holding and swept my gaze around the inner courtyard. It was barren except for a statue of a sword. A green vine with black roses wound around it. Not having a whole lot of time to examine it, I scanned the walls, noticing that several doors were on each and pondered which one I should enter. None of them really called to me.

Near the back of the courtyard, I could see a set of stone stairs leading up to a third floor, and directly at the top of the stairs was an ornate doorway. Two dark wooden doors with metal studs and brackets stood open, a soft, glowing light filtering from the darkness within. As I stared at those doors, I began to feel the energy pulsing through the air, and the hairs on my arms stood up.

Rushing toward the steps, I took them two at a time until I was standing in front of the doorway, breathing heavily. Inside, a fire glowed in the middle of a vast room. Despite the light coming from the flames, the space was shadowed in darkness. I steeled myself for traps that might be in there because there would be. I was sure of it. There was no way this was going to be easy. Anyway, who would magick a castle to keep people out, and then make it easy to get the treasure?

No one, that was who.

Man, I wish I had my flashlight with me, or Teagan's spell to make light.

As I crept into the room, my body tensed, just waiting for something to jump out at me. No matter how hard I tried, I couldn't see into the shadows, so I kept my eyes focused on the fire in front of me. The flames licked the ceiling, crackling and spewing sparks into the air. The energy that I had felt in the courtyard intensified with each step I took closer to it. The heat wasn't what I had expected; it was warm but not unbearably so. It was a magical fire but nonetheless would burn me if I got too close.

I kept approaching, wary and alert. When I was within fifteen feet of the flames, I realized that it was a ring of fire, and through it, I could see a slab of stone with a large book on top of it. Magic pulsed like music in the air from the book, and I felt the pull to go to it grow stronger. I took a few more steps closer, the heat becoming more intense as I tried to figure out how I was going to get through it to the book.

A rustling noise came from the darkness on my right and I instantly went into defensive mode with my hands out in front of me. I couldn't quite make out what it was, but the distinct sound of something sliding across the floor had my mind in overdrive.

I didn't have to wait long before an enormous black snake slithered around the circle of fire, hissing and baring its fangs at me. I jumped back, startled, and my instant thought was to run, but I couldn't. Frantically, I searched around for some kind of weapon, but there was none. All I had was my fledgling magic. Magic I hadn't yet mastered and really had no idea how to work.

The monster snake had red eyes that glowed in the firelight, making it look even more menacing if that was even possible. It seemed to stare right into my soul as it settled down, curling around the fire as if the heat didn't bother it at all. Black scales rippled over the length of it like armor.

Guess I'm going to have to wing it like before. If I died, so be it, but at least I tried.

As I began to gather what energy I had left after dissolving the shield outside, I felt the magic from the book pulsing toward me. The snake lifted its head up from where it rested, hissing. It did not like me doing that. Lunging at me, I screamed, throwing what power I had at it as hard as I could.

And absolutely nothing happened.

Fear bubbled up in me as the creature loomed, ready to strike. I couldn't move fast enough, and I knew this was the end. I had failed.

A screech sounded behind me, and just as the snake moved to bite, a black body slammed into its head, knocking it away from me. Slashing and tearing at the snake, the figure went berserk on it, and then another black figure joined in. Growling and hissing, they attacked the snake with precision, causing the snake to not know which figure to attack first.

Back and forth it went until black blood began to flow from the gouges and ripped areas of the snake's body. Within only a few minutes, the battle was over, and the snake slumped to the ground before dissolving into black smoke that drifted away over the flames.

The black figures pranced over to me, and in the firelight, I could see that my saviors were Charlie and Emric. I had never been so relieved.

My arms shook, and I fought back the tears as I dropped to my knees beside them, reaching out to hug both around the neck. "Thank you," I whispered to them as I got myself under control.

"You're never alone, Andie. Even when you think you are. We know when you need us," Emric purred. I rubbed a hand over his head. *I think I prefer their panther forms, but I won't tell them that.*

"As much as I'd like to be tough about all of this, I really thought I was a goner. I'm honestly surprised I didn't pee my pants."

They both chuckled and rubbed against me.

"Where are the others? Please tell me they're okay?" I asked quickly, a different type of fear invading my heart.

"They are hurt, but not dead. Teagan and Killian are in the courtyard where we left them. They will sleep for a while with the magic we wove over them to help them heal. Right now, it's just us. Freya is not dead, but she was wounded before she fled. Teagan and Killian killed the rest of her group before she took off," Charlie said.

Relief warred with the need to rush out there and check on them myself, but I knew that Emric and Charlie wouldn't let anything happen to them.

"Thank you for taking such good care of them, guys. I can't tell you how much of a relief that is to hear. I don't trust Freya to not try to stop me, even if she is hurt. So... any thoughts on how to get through this fire?" I asked them, hopeful they had the answer.

They glanced at each other, then back at me, and I knew that they didn't have any great ideas. How in the heck was I supposed to get to a magic book standing in a ring of fire? There had to be some trick, some magic words. *Something!*

Emric cleared his throat and sat in front of me, his yellow eyes sad as they looked into mine. "I'm sorry, Andie. There is no other way through the fire except to walk right into it. It has been magicked so that no counter spell can weaken or diminish it. This will be your greatest trial yet."

I knew his words were true; he wouldn't lie to me. I stared into the fire, knowing that if I walked through it, I would be burned badly, the pain from my previous dream even more terrifying in reality. I knew I might not make it, especially since I would have to walk through once to get the book, and then back out again. But here I was. I was meant to get the treasures, at least that was what everyone told me. I had to trust that Emric and Charlie would take care of me and heal me from whatever happened to me next.

I couldn't think. I just had to do it.

Taking a deep breath, I imagined that I was on that mountain again, silence surrounding me, and a soft, cool breeze blew over my skin. And then I took a step. And then another. Before I knew it, I was two feet away from the fire, the heat almost too much to stand. I closed my eyes and bit my lip as I pushed myself to hurry through the flames, steeling myself for the pain that would follow.

I waited for it—I was ready. But I felt no heat. I felt no pain at all as I passed right through.

Wonder filled me as I ran to the book, picking it up from the cold slab. It came off easily, and a melody tinkled in the air. As I held it to my chest, the adrenaline still high, it shook and wiggled against me. A glow came from the knotted symbol on the front of it as I held it away from me. Before my eyes, the book slowly transformed into an intricate silver sword, the symbol welded in the middle. The weight from it tugged my arm down, but I found I could easily heft it back up.

The Sword of Light! The first treasure to be found of the Tuatha De Danann. I held it reverently, studying every inch of it as the fire roared around me. I couldn't believe I had done it. How had I not gotten burnt? The heat was real, but the fire hadn't touched me! Feeling more confident, I grasped the hilt of the sword and turned back to where Emric and Charlie both sat, watching me with smug looks on their panther faces.

Those rascals! Somehow, they knew that I would be okay.

I walked faster this time through the fire, and after I passed through the bright flames, the sword began to wiggle and shake again, this time transforming back into the book, only into a smaller version that fit in the palm of my hand.

Well, that's handy, I thought as I slipped it into a pocket over my heart where I knew it would be safe. I patted it gently and knew that I would continue to do so until we got it back where it belonged.

"You two have some explaining to do." I plopped down on the ground in front of them, exhausted from all the emotions that I had gone through in one day.

"We obviously couldn't tell you if it would burn you or not. We really did not know. Legend has always been that the one who would save us would be able to walk through the fire with nary an injury. Anyone else would burst into flames to join the rest of the fire in protecting it. Luckily that was not you, yes?" Charlie said.

"Yes. Lucky it wasn't me," I agreed.

After I had gotten my wits back to me and caught my breath, the three of us went to find Teagan and Killian. Both were still out of it and looked horrible. Gashes and bruises covered their bodies, and I cringed. The panthers assured me that they would be fine before slinging the teens over their backs, and we took off out of the castle. I followed them to a spot in the courtyard that I hadn't noticed when I first came in. Had it even been there? Who knew? Things were never as they seemed here.

There stood a doorway that was made of branches in the form of a circle. It had to be the circular doorway that Coeus mentioned. If what he said was correct, we would be able to walk through it, think about where we wanted to go while we did, and we would end up there on the other side. I guess Emric and Charlie had the same idea because they sauntered up to it stepping right through without a thought. Emric called over his shoulder. "Tell it you want to go back to Aine's Oak Tree."

And that was just what I did.

As I stepped through, I promptly fell out the other side, landing hard on my hands and knees. I brushed the hair back from my eyes and looked up to see Aine, Celeste, and all the fairies gathered around inside the oak tree, waiting on us. Balwyn and Eira ran around the room making sure everyone had drinks and snacks. Many different emotions showed on their faces. Glee that we had gotten the treasure. Worry about Killian and Teagan, and confusion when they noticed that one of our group was missing. My heart ached as Hunter's absence finally had a chance to hit me.

Aine and the fairies directed Charlie and Emric to take the boys to get healed and rested, and as I held back my tears at the thought of Hunter, Celeste came over and helped me up, pulling me into her arms and holding me tightly. The dam fell, and all the tears that I had held back for so long welled over, and I sobbed. Because of me, he was dead.

Celeste rubbed my back and hair, gently murmuring into my ear words meant to soothe. When the tears began to dry up, and all I could manage was to hiccup, she set me back from her, looking into my eyes with a serious expression.

"What happened was not your fault, Andie. Not at all. You cannot let your mind trick you into thinking that. You know it's not what Hunter would want. And for all you know, he may still be alive. I've got someone looking into it, I promise."

My emotions were all over the place, but I knew I had to get the book to where it belonged. Hiccupping again, I wiped my runny nose and eyes, then reached into my pocket. Pulling out the book, I told her about the larger version changing into the sword, and then back into this smaller book. She patted my hand and leaned in to kiss my cheek.

"I know just where it needs to go. Come."

Chapter Eighteen

The next few days were a whirlwind of activity within the fairy community. Celeste had whisked us back to her house, where she pulled out the large book I always caught her reading and the one that Aine used to talk to as "Anne." When she opened it, she whispered a few words while holding the miniature book over it. Sparks and magical energy exploded from the treasure before completely disappearing from her hands. Before I was able to exclaim, she pointed down to the large book in front of us. As my eyes landed on it, I saw that where there had previously been a blank page sat the first treasure.

To someone unfamiliar with the treasures, the book would have looked just like any book. This particular page might seem a bit odd, with only the picture of one book in the top corner, no passage or words, but no one else would suspect what it was if they were to open it.

Who would think to look for a priceless treasure inside of a book? I certainly wouldn't have.

Celeste glanced up at Teagan, Killian, and I as she reverently closed the book and took it to her large bookshelf, sliding it in between a million others. We watched as she gestured with her hands, speaking words that would seal it there as an extra measure of security.

I sighed as I stared at it, sitting there so obscure amid all the great works that it sat beside. I wished Hunter could have been here to see what he helped accomplish, because there was no way I could have gotten this key without him or the rest of my group. I was still raw with emotion when it came to thinking about him. I wasn't ready to give up and let myself believe that he was dead. Not until Celeste's friends confirmed it would I give up hope. I know he wouldn't have given up easily on me.

As if reading my mind, Teagan squeezed my hand, and I was grateful for his strength and friendship. We still had three more Keys to find, and each new journey would be more treacherous than the one before.

Late that night, I sat on the end of Killian's bed as he asked a lot of questions about my childhood. Celeste had prepared one of her extra rooms for him since he had nowhere else to go. He was in awe of the television and ceiling fan, and when he had sat on the bed, his eyes rolled back in pleasure.

The village he had been born in and lived his entire life was nothing like what I had experienced growing up. He might as well have been living in medieval times. The bed he had slept on was a pallet of straw wrapped in fabric, and he had never experienced running water. It blew my mind and made me happy that he was able to experience such small things that gave him pleasure now.

We talked until we were both yawning. The clock showed that it was two in the morning. As I said goodnight and turned to walk out of his room, Celeste burst in, her long white nightgown swirling around her feet in her hurry. Her face was severe, and my throat closed with dread. I knew that whatever the news was, it wasn't good.

"They found him."

-To Be Continued in Book Two

Acknowledgements

There are so many people to thank for their help with seeing this book come to fruition. Thank you to the very patient and talented Maria Spada for designing a beautiful cover that was exactly what I envisioned and more. To my editor, Lindsay York. Her patience and beautiful editing know no bounds.

To my husband and sons, for their patience when I was deep into the writing process, and their encouragement and love when I was uncertain.

About the Author

J.C. Lucas lives in North Texas with her husband and three sons, and spending time with her sweet grandson. She loves to read, garden, and watch the hummingbirds when she is not writing about worlds of fantasy and intrigue.